UNTAMED

IVY JACKSON

Copyright © 2023 by Ivy Jackson

All rights reserved.

No part of this book may be reproduced in any form or by any electronic or mechanical means, including information storage and retrieval systems, without written permission from the author, except for the use of brief quotations in a book review.

Discreet Cover Designer: Jillian Liota at Blue Moon Creative Studio

Model: Forest

Model Photographer: Wander Aguiar Photography

Editing: Sandra at One Love Editing

Formatting: Victoria at Cruel Ink Editing + Design

Proofreading: Victoria at Cruel Ink Editing + Design

DEDICATION

To all my girlies who love a man on their knees.

A NOTE ABOUT THE CONTENT OF UNTAMED

This books contains discussions about grief due to loss of a loved one which happens in the past, off page. This book also takes place mainly on a ranch that has an animal rescue on it. There is very brief talk about animal cruelty.

A PLAYLIST TO GET YOU IN YOUR COWBOY ERA

"Stuck Like Glue" - Sugarland

"Pontoon" - Little Big Town

"Hurricane" - Luke Combs

"All Your'n" - Tyler Childers

"She Thinks My Tractor's Sexy" - Trace Adkins

"1,2 Many" - Luke Combs and Brooks & Dunn

"Stay" - Sugarland

CHAPTER ONE

River

"SURPRISED TO SEE YOU HERE, DARLIN'."

My entire body freezes. I should've known there would be no way I could escape this moment. Ever since I moved back to town, I've been avoiding him like the plague. But since his brother basically forced me to come back to their ranch in order to adopt one of their rescue dogs, I knew he'd find me like a damn heat-seeking missile.

I've successfully avoided him all day, sneaking around the barn with all the rescues while he worked and then hanging out with his brother Rhett's girlfriend all afternoon. But when Poppy begged me to come to her birthday bonfire, I knew it was a bad idea. I tried to get out of it, knowing that Hayes would find me, but she looked stressed about her fight with Rhett and was so hopeful that I would come keep her company.

I caved.

But I refuse to look in his direction, instead focusing on the grape salad that's in front of me. I was trying to fill my plate with the sweet marshmallow and brown sugar stuff before he decided to drop in. And now I'm just…frozen. My arm is outstretched over the table filled with food, and my fingers dig hard into the plate I'm holding.

"I'm sure you are." My voice finally comes, but it's unsure and quiet. I haven't spoken to him in over a decade. Not since we fought. Not since I told him I never wanted to see him again. "And don't call me darlin'," I add. Because that's what he always called me, even when we were kids.

And my heart can't take that kind of ache.

"Right?" he asks. "Because I'm pretty sure the last thing you said to me was that you never wanted to see my narcissistic, hypocritical, smug-ass face again." He hums like he's thinking hard about it. "Did I miss anything?"

"Ugly."

"Ouch."

I shrug. "Leave me alone, Hayes. I'm only here because your brother practically dragged me."

"Which one?"

I sigh. He knows which one. Rhett is too grumpy to speak to anyone but Poppy. Dean is in rehab — at least, that's the last I heard. And Wells is the one I'm still friendly with. He knows it was Wells, and the fact that he's just trying to get more of my attention is annoying as hell.

"Wells." My voice comes out cold and hostile. Good. I want him to leave me alone.

"Why would Wells drag you here?"

"God, can't you ever do as you're fucking told? Just respect people's boundaries and walk the fuck away." My temper spills over, and I instantly regret it because when I finally turn to face him, I'm assaulted with memories of us. It's like a car crash I can't look away from. His dirty-blond hair is hanging out from under his black cowboy hat, and his blue eyes look ornery as hell in this firelight. That little smirk on his lips makes me want to kick him in the shins.

"River—" he starts.

"I've been wanting a dog." I decide just to tell him as quickly as I can. The faster I quell his curiosity, the faster he'll leave me alone. "And Wells wouldn't help me rescue one until I came out to the ranch to see him and your momma and pops. Then Poppy begged me to come out to her birthday party, and I caved. Because she's sweet and new here, and I'd like to be her friend. I didn't come here for you, or to talk to you, so just leave. Me. Alone."

"You're gettin' a dog?"

"Yes," I grind out. God, I didn't think it would sting this much to be around him. "And I'll have to come out here every day for a while. Because Betty has to get used to me before I can take her home. I'll try to make sure I'm only here while you're out working so we won't cross paths."

He scoffs and crosses his arms over his broad chest. I try really, really hard not to get distracted by his forearms. They were always the object of my fixation. From years of playing guitar and working on the ranch, they're strong and tan, and my fucking god I'm distracted.

"Don't put yourself out on my account."

"What? What do you want from me, Hayes? I wasn't kidding when I said I never wanted to see you again. Why would you think that had changed?"

"Why'd you move back here, then?"

"Oh, my god."

I laugh, but I don't find it funny. I'm angry. I'm angry at him and my mom and the fact that I can't run to Addie because she's gone, and this place feels so fucking empty without her.

Tossing my plate down on the table and losing a few grapes in the process, I lean in toward him. We're surrounded by people talking, music playing, and the bonfire crackling, but I still don't want to draw attention to us. I'm sure his parents know something happened because I was here every damn day of my childhood, running around this ranch, trying to keep up with the boys and then playing with Addie in the evenings.

I don't want them to know what happened. The embarrassment would end me.

"I came home because my momma needed me to help her with bills." I couldn't say no. No matter how shitty of a mother she was to me, I couldn't let her starve or lose the house. And it's not like my sister, Janie, could just leave her job and husband in New York. "Coming back to Cane Creek had nothing to do with you, Hayes. I dreaded it. I loved my life in Bozeman, and I knew if I came back here, I would run into you no matter how hard I tried to avoid it. But Momma needed me, and I couldn't say no."

I can feel the tightness in my throat that always comes with crying. But I will not break down here, not in front of him. He is no longer my rock or my best friend. He is no longer my confidant.

"So why not just send her money from Bozeman?"

I sigh. "I wasn't making enough. I was barely making enough to support myself there. I had to come home."

Spilling my guts to him feels familiar and gives me a small sense of relief. I don't want it to, but it does. There will always be a piece of me that feels comforted by him.

"I'm sorry, River. That has to be tough. I know you had big dreams."

My big dreams involved him and only him. He was all I wanted. Anything else was just a happy bonus. I would've stayed here and lived a peaceful life on the ranch. I love this place. It wouldn't have been a hardship to live this life with him.

"I don't need your sympathy, Hayes. I just need you to leave me alone. Please."

"I'm sorry that bein' around me is such a pain for you, darlin'."

I can feel my entire body flush red with anger. And I'm really about to give him a piece of my mind when he opens his stupid mouth again, crushing me all over again.

"Most women don't find it so difficult."

Breathing deeply, I close my eyes for a moment, smiling even though I feel anything but happy at this moment. He's winding me up on purpose, and I refuse to feed into this game he's playing. I lick my lips and then look back up at him.

"Alright, Hayes. We get it." I pick my plate up and add one more scoop of grapes. "You're a fuckboy, and you have women throwing themselves all over you. So go get one of them to give you the attention you crave. I am not going to be that person for you anymore."

I pop a grape in my mouth and then walk away, leaving him to stand there alone like the asshole he is. Looking over to where Poppy was when I left her, I see her cuddled up to Rhett while his kids eat their plates of food that I helped them pile high with sweets. I am definitely not interrupting that little moment.

So instead, I go over to Wells. He greets me with his warm, signature smile and wraps an arm around my shoulders, shaking me lightly as he hugs me.

"Hayes botherin' you?"

I laugh, chewing on another grape. The marshmallow cream and brown sugar combination makes my teeth hurt in the best way.

"When isn't he bothering me?"

I refuse to look back at him, but Wells doesn't. Wells looks over my shoulder, grinning, and then fucking winks at him. These men. They've always known how to pester the shit out of each other, pushing buttons until they're fighting with their fists in the backyard. Clyde had to break them up once when Hayes pissed Rhett off so badly he left Hayes with a broken nose and a bloody lip.

"Don't start," I tell him, a warning tone to my voice.

"What?" He looks down at me, smiling wide with falsely innocent eyes.

"Don't 'what' me, Wells Black. I know how y'all work. Leave it be."

He kisses the side of my head, and I fight the urge to look at Hayes for the rest of the night.

CHAPTER TWO

Hayes

"WHAT TIME IS RIVER COMIN' over today?"

Everyone in the kitchen goes quiet. Never knew it was so easy to get my family to shut up. I'll have to mention her name more often.

"I know one of y'all knows." I pointedly look from Wells to Rhett to my pops. Momma already went over to Rhett's house to take care of the kids, and I know I would be able to get an answer from her.

"I'm sure Poppy knows," Wells says, grinning into his coffee cup.

"Don't get my woman involved," Rhett all but growls. "And we have a lot of work to do today. I can't have you runnin' off to pester River all day."

"Where's Poppy?" I ask, ignoring Rhett's grumpy mood.

"Getting things up and running over in the rescue

barn. It's her turn to start early." Wells finishes the rest of his coffee and sets it upside down on the top shelf of the dishwasher. "But I should really get over there and start helpin'."

Rhett grunts.

"What time is River coming?" I try again, but both Rhett and Wells leave me hanging, walking out of the house without another word.

"Are we gonna have a problem?" Pops asks once we're alone, giving his newspaper a little shake before looking at me over the edge. His reading glasses slip down his nose.

I just give him a questioning look, raising an eyebrow.

"I don't know what happened between you two, but I don't want you to bother her when she's just tryin' to adopt that sweet pup."

"I made a mistake that I'm trying to own up to," I tell him.

"Pretty big mistake to keep her away for so long," he says.

I know what he's getting at — the fact that I fucked up so royally that she couldn't even feel comfortable enough to come home for Addie's funeral.

"Mhm," I hum.

This shit hits me like a punch to the gut. River and Addie were pretty close, always hanging out when River got tired of chasin' after us boys all day. I never reached out to her when the crap with Addie was happening because it's a small town and her momma would've known and told her. If River didn't want to come home for that, she didn't want to come home. Me bugging her about it would've only had her coming home out of some weird guilt. Because who can say no to the brother of a dying girl?

I wanted her to come back because she *wanted* to. Not because I begged her to. It broke my heart thinking that she wasn't coming back to say goodbye to Addie just because I was around. It made me angry that she would be so petty. But my baby sister was dying, so leaving room in my heart and mind for River to occupy wasn't really on the top of my list.

But through all of that, I still missed my best friend. When Addie left us and we had to put her in the ground, I needed River. I needed her through that whole damn thing, and she was just off living her best life in the city. I missed her so much it was a physical ache in my bones.

I bite back the anger that threatens to rise up because I did it to myself. I pushed her away. I made her so uncomfortable to be on this damn ranch that she couldn't even come say goodbye to Addie. I did that.

I shrug. "I dunno, Pops. That woman is stubborn."

"Ah!" He folds the paper and tosses it on the table, pointing a finger in my direction. "Don't discount her like that. You break her heart?"

God, this family is nosy as hell.

"None of your business."

"It is my business when it's happening on my ranch. What happened between you two, son?"

I've come to terms with the shit that happened between River and me over the last decade, and how I ruined everything when it came to our friendship, and whatever the hell else we had going for us. But hashing that all out with my pops is not something that's on my agenda today…or anytime soon.

Admitting how childish I was to myself is one thing, but saying it out loud is a whole other ball game.

"Nothin'." I throw back the rest of my coffee. "Better get goin'. Rhett won't take kindly to me dawdling."

"Look."

"Here we go." I lean against the counter and look at where he's turned around in his chair. I was so close to making it out the door.

"Don't sass me, kid. You may be grown, but I'll still kick your ass."

I mimic zipping my lips and throwing away the key.

"She'll probably be popping by when she gets off this afternoon from the vet's. And it'll be a relatively small window of time because I heard from a good source that she's at the bar tonight." He clears his throat, picks up his paper, and turns back around. "You didn't hear that from me."

I grin like a cat that got the fuckin' cream.

"Thanks, Pops."

He just gives me a wave over his head.

"Don't fuck it up this time!" he shouts as the screen door thwacks shut.

I don't intend to.

When I saw her standing back on this ranch, her pretty, tanned skin lit up by firelight, it felt like everything just *clicked* back into place. Like I've been missin' a part of my life that was supposed to be here the entire time.

And, hot damn, when she turned that firecracker attitude onto me, I damn near fell to my knees. I'll take all the anger she has if that's what it costs to get her to talk to me again.

CHAPTER THREE

River

"RIVER?"

I jolt out of my thoughts and suddenly remember where I am — cutting the incontinence tablets in half for poor Sadie. Her mom brought her in today wearing a diaper, and I don't think I've ever seen a dog look more embarrassed.

"Sorry. Yeah?"

I look over my shoulder to find my coworker, Cheryl, raising an eyebrow at me and tapping her toe. She is the epitome of a grumpy front desk worker — a *Karen*, if you will.

"You going to be done with that anytime soon?" She nods to the pills on the counter. "They've been waiting forever."

"They've been waiting for five minutes," I mumble

under my breath, turning back to the counter to make sure I'm giving them the right amount.

"What was that?"

"Nothing, Cheryl." I sigh, push the pills into the plastic bottle, and hand it over to her. My shift is almost over, and I don't have the energy to fight with her today. Especially not over how long it takes me to cut up some pills when all she does is paint her damn nails up there. I don't even think she likes animals.

I check my watch, and seeing that I only have about five minutes left, I quickly clean up my mess and run through the checklist on the clipboard hanging from the wall.

"Hey! Sorry, I'm late! I know! I'm hurrying!" Evie dashes past me, running at lightning speed to get to the back room.

"You're fine!" I call after her, laughing quietly when I hear her run into something. A loud crash and a lot of swear words later, she's leaning against the doorframe, red-faced and breathing heavily. She looks like she's been crying, and my amusement turns to worry.

"You alright?" I take a few steps toward her, laying my hand on her shoulder. She bites her lip and smiles, blinking hard.

"Yeah." She sighs. "Just not a good start to the day."

"You want me to stay for you? I really don't have anything I can't miss until the bar tonight."

"Don't be silly!" She waves me off, trying her

hardest to smile, even though I can see it's difficult. She's hiding something, but we aren't close enough for me to expect her to talk to me. Sure, we work together here and there, but if something is wrong, I wouldn't expect to be the first person she ran to.

"The only way I will leave you when something is clearly wrong is if you promise me that you will call me if you feel like you can't hang. Yeah?"

I make sure she's looking at me when she agrees. She's a pretty thing, all legs with long, blonde hair and green eyes. She nods and tries smiling again, so I change the subject as I start to clock out.

"Cheryl is on one today," I tell her. "So tread lightly if you have to go up front."

"When isn't she?" She groans. "Who's the doctor on staff today?"

"Martinez."

"Thank god. Should be an easy day, then." She checks her phone and then shoves it into her back pocket. "Where you off to now?"

"Well," I tell her, smiling because I'm so freaking excited that I get to go see my girl. "I'm actually working on adopting a dog. But she needs some extra love, so I'll be going out to spend time with her until she's ready to come home with me."

"Oh, that's awesome!" Her smile is genuine now, and it makes her whole face light up. "Where you gettin' her from?"

"Wells Black, from that rescue he and his brothers run out on the ranch."

Her face drops all its color, and I'm about to make sure she isn't going to faint when Cheryl storms into the back.

"I've been callin' you about Teddy! He's here for a damn nail trim!"

"Shit, sorry, Cheryl," Evie says, running her hands over the front of her shirt. "I'm getting him now."

"Hey, remember what I said." I grab her arm before she makes it out front.

"I will. I promise."

And then she's off to grab Teddy from reception. I have no clue what's going on with her, but I'm definitely going to make sure my phone is on me for the rest of the afternoon.

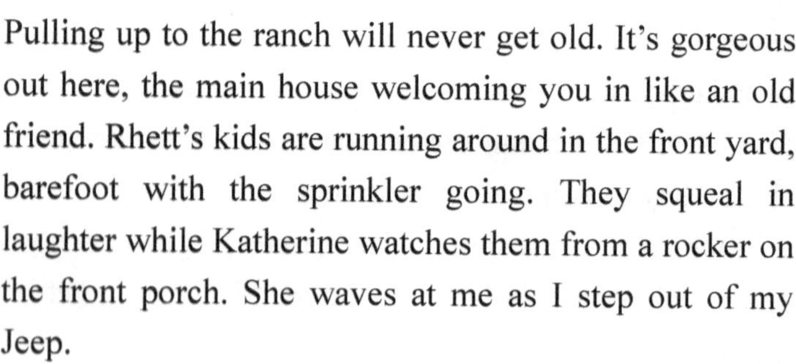

Pulling up to the ranch will never get old. It's gorgeous out here, the main house welcoming you in like an old friend. Rhett's kids are running around in the front yard, barefoot with the sprinkler going. They squeal in laughter while Katherine watches them from a rocker on the front porch. She waves at me as I step out of my Jeep.

"Hi, sweet girl!" she calls out. "Wells is waitin' for you in the barn!"

"Thanks, Katherine!" I look around, waiting for Hayes to jump out of the bushes. I know he's got to be lurking around here somewhere. I'm sure no matter how hard everyone has tried to respect my wishes, someone has let it slip that I'm going to be here today.

"Yeah, he knows," she says, at least looking a little ashamed of herself. "I don't know who told him — they're all pleading the fifth. But if I had to guess, I'd blame Clyde."

"Don't pin that on me, woman!" I hear Clyde shout from inside. I bite my cheek to keep from laughing. Katherine just shrugs and smiles, leaning her head back and closing her eyes as a breeze blows over the front lawn.

God, it's gorgeous here. They have the perfect piece of land. The mountains sit as a gorgeous backdrop to the fields and old trees. There's even a creek that runs through the back of the property that I may or may not have skinny-dipped in a few times in my youth.

I take a deep breath, taking in the sounds of home, and then stalk off in the direction of the barn. I am hoping and praying the entire way that Hayes is not sittin' inside that barn when I get in there. I still have flashbacks to the last time I saw him, before Poppy's party, when he was so drunk he could barely stand up. He threw up on the drive back and mumbled some things I think would make him die of embarrassment if he heard it repeated back.

And I still don't think he knows about that night — when the whole world was collapsing in on him, and I found out too late. His dad had to carry him upstairs, and I cried the entire drive home.

It's almost enough to make the drama that happened between us seem…insignificant. Like maybe I should get over it and get over myself and just be friends with him again. Maybe I just need to suck it up and be there for him like I wasn't able to be when he needed it.

But then I remember the way he *screamed* at me at high school graduation, and I change my mind.

"Hey, friend!" Poppy calls out when she sees me. "I was just thinking it was about time for you to get here. How was work?"

"It was good." I shrug. "A bit slow today. But knowing I was coming out here to see my girl, Betty, made it go faster."

"I gave her a bath this morning," she tells me, walking by my side as we slowly approach Betty's little room. "She hated it, but she smells like oatmeal now."

"Hi there, baby girl!" My voice is high-pitched and happy, trying to assure her that I'm only there to love on her. That whip of a tail slowly moves back and forth while her ears are tucked back against her head.

"She wants to be excited so bad." Poppy's voice is a bit sad. "But she's still hesitant."

"We'll work on it," I assure her. "I'm not going to give up on her. I promise."

She nods and opens the door, and I sit down on the cool concrete, my legs stretched out in front of me to block her exit.

"Care if I sit with you for a bit? Wells is off making some calls about getting in some new pups, so I may as well take advantage of him being gone and chill."

I laugh. "Of course not. But I don't think I would be scared of Wells getting upset with you sitting down if I were you."

"Psh." She sits down slowly and leans against the wall. "I'm not afraid of him, just don't want anyone to feel like I'm slacking off now that I'm boning the boss."

I snort, and Betty's ears instinctively raise up.

"What?" Poppy's face is a picture of mock innocence. She's trying her hardest not to laugh. "I am."

"Gross." I make a face at her. "I grew up with these boys. Rhett is practically my brother. They all are." *Liar.* "I don't want to hear about his sex life."

"Me either." Hayes pops in out of nowhere, and I can feel my body physically react to his presence. It's a strange mixture of desire and anger.

I sigh.

"Hi, Hayes."

CHAPTER FOUR

River

"HEY THERE, DARLIN'."

His grin is wide as he saunters his way over to us, the guitar pick rolling between his lips. I used to watch his tongue flick and twist that thing all the time back in high school, fascinated with the way his mouth moved.

"Who told you?" Poppy whips around to look him over with a really impressive stink eye.

"I'm takin' that to my grave, peachy Poppy."

Taking the pick out of his mouth, he plays with it between his fingers instead. I don't know if it's just a Hayes thing or if I just really like hands, but as his strong fingers play with that little piece of plastic, they make the muscles in his forearms jump, and I find myself staring far too blatantly.

Poppy groans and rolls her eyes. "We're having a girls' day, and no one wants you here."

"That's hurtful." His hand clutches his chest over his heart. "Especially when all I did was come in here to tell you that Rhett is taking the afternoon off."

"He's what now?"

Oh no. Her resolve is failing.

"Taking the afternoon off. Said something about alone time without the kids? Or something?" Hayes shrugs, but I *know* this is all part of some master plan to get our chaperone out of the barn.

"Clever," I tell him.

"I won't go if you don't want me to." She's lowered her voice, speaking just to me. And while I wish I could keep her here, I'm not going to be the lame reason my new friend doesn't get laid. "Actually, no. I'm not going. You Black boys can quit with the scheming."

"Poppy, it's fine." I smile at her and nudge her thigh with my boot. "Go to your man."

She looks back and forth between us. I nudge her again.

"Go. I've been dealing with this one since I was a kid." I nod my head in Hayes' direction, chancing a look at him. But he's just standing there, leaning against the wall with his arms crossed and a very up-to-no-good looking smirk on his face. "I'll handle him."

"I sure hope you will."

"Don't be gross," Poppy chides him as she gets up off the floor. "Be respectful, or I'll come back in here and kick your ass. Roger?"

Her finger is pressed into his chest, but he doesn't move. Just looks down at her with that same little grin.

"Yes, ma'am."

"I mean it, Hayes. I'm not above siccing Rhett on your ass."

We both watch her leave, her pace picking up the farther away from us she gets. That girl is head over heels for Rhett, and I don't blame her for wanting to take advantage of what little alone time they have.

"Think Betty would let me sit here with you?"

I lean my head back on the wall behind me and slowly look him over. It doesn't matter if I say no; he's going to plop his cute little butt down on the floor next to me. There's no getting out of it. I have to be here for Betty, so I gesture to the ground across from me.

Betty's ears go back as she scoots closer to the newcomer, her pink nose sniffing him out.

"Hey, old girl." His hand slowly moves toward her, his palm up so she can sniff it. She must be used to him hanging around because instead of cozying up to me, she lies down next to him, her head just barely touching his leg.

"Should've known you'd get it out of someone. Next time, I'll be sure to tell Poppy to keep it to herself."

"Truce, River?" He shoves his guitar pick in his pocket and crosses his legs at the ankles. He looks the picture of relaxed, but I know this has to be just as uncomfortable for him as it is for me. No one likes to be around their ex-best friend. It's awkward as hell, and when you both left on angry terms…

Yeah, just not fun.

"Depends for how long."

"Riv." He laughs, but it's void of all humor. "I don't wanna keep fightin' with you. You're back in town, and the love I had for you is still there. So can we just call a truce and move on?"

"Hayes, I'll call a truce, and I'll be civil, but I'm not your best friend anymore. The things you said to me…"

"I know." He has the good sense to look ashamed. "Can we maybe talk about it?"

"No." I'm not ready to go down that road, and I don't know if I ever will be. I think the time for him to apologize has passed. He should've reached out to me before I left or while I was gone. But I never heard from him, so it just feels a little forced at this point. Like he's only apologizing because there's no escaping me.

"I'd like to apologize, River."

"I don't want your apology, Hayes."

"God, you're just as stubborn. That sure as shit hasn't changed."

That gets a laugh out of me.

"No, it has not." I shake my head slowly, smiling down at Betty because I refuse to give him any more of my happiness.

"I missed that, you know."

"My stubbornness?" I ask, lifting my face to his.

"Your smile."

"God, Hayes." I groan, but I can't help that it makes my smile grow even wider. He's such a little shit. Always flirting where he has no business doing so. "You're so annoying."

"Because I make you smile?" His face is scrunched up in mock confusion. "Normally, that's seen as a good thing, Riv."

"God, fuck off," I tease him, shoving his thigh with my boot. "Your flirting will get you nowhere with me."

"I'm not flirting."

"Yes, you are. I'd recognize it anywhere."

"River," he says, his voice low as he leans in toward me. His arms are crossed, and I don't like the way my eyes trail down to his bulging biceps. "When I flirt with you, you'll know it."

He knows exactly how to throw me off my game, making me hot and uncomfortable at the same time. I stare at him for a second, and he relishes in it, putting on his best sexy smile.

"Shouldn't you be getting back to work?" I avoid his eye contact by watching Betty scoot even closer to Hayes when I try to pet her. "Especially with Rhett being...unavailable? Because you're messing up my bonding time. She seems to be liking you more than me."

"Yeah." He chuckles. "She's a good girl. I spend a

lot of time in here playing guitar and chatting with Poppy while she waits for Rhett to finish up at the end of the day."

"Still the slacker?" I ask him.

He grunts, and his demeanor changes.

"I'm not a slacker, Riv. I'm just tired of not being able to do what I want with my life. Hell, you know how it is. You were livin' it up in the big city, having fun and doing what you wanted. Only to come back here because your mom needed you?" He shakes his head and twirls Betty's ear between his fingers. "Shit sucks."

"Still wanting to play your music?"

"Don't care about makin' it big or even leaving the ranch. But with Dean out of commission, we're left strapped for help."

"How long's he been gone?"

"I think the easier question is how long he's actually been around. But even then, when he was here, he wasn't *here*. Dean hasn't been here since we were teenagers."

"I'm sorry, Hayes." I feel for this whole damn family and the shit that Dean has put them through. I know it's been tough on all of them.

"Yeah." He shrugs. "Rhett won't come out with how bad things are actually lookin', but I know he's stressed. Hiring Poppy on wasn't even his idea. Pops forced his hand on it."

"So you spending less time working on the ranch is out of the question."

He clicks his tongue. "Bingo."

I'm going to regret this, but fuck if I'm not a sucker for this man being sad. He's already been through enough, and maybe sitting here with him for a couple of hours a day won't be all bad. Betty seems to like him well enough; maybe he can help me gain her trust and love.

"Alright." I sigh. "You can stay. The truce will extend to my visits here and here only. But on one condition."

"I let you hold my hand?"

"No." I laugh.

"You want a kiss?" He wags his eyebrows.

"Shut up, Hayes. No. You help me win this one over." I nod in Betty's direction. "Do that, and I'll let you hang out with me when I come over."

"*Let me*," he repeats. "You think you could stop me, darlin'?"

"I think your brothers could. Or Clyde. Or Katherine." I give him a pointed look.

"Message received. I'll help you with Betty, you help me escape Drill Sergeant Black."

He extends his hand, and I stare at it for a moment before reaching out and clasping it in my own. His hands are rough and warm, and I can feel the foundation of the walls I built beginning to crack. He's going to weasel his way in one day at a time.

If I'm going to survive this, we're going to have to fast-track this trust-gaining experience.

CHAPTER FIVE

Hayes

"YOU PLANNIN' on just wearin' her down?" Rhett asks between his ax hitting the stump of wood over and over again. It finally cracks, splitting right down the middle.

I grab one and get to work because being so close to River the other day has my nerves on edge. The way she smelled and the way she smiled. Christ, I haven't seen her smile at me in far too long. I've missed it. And now that I've had a taste, I'm desperate for it. She's all I've been thinking about for the last few days. Especially since I haven't been able to escape work to go see her and Betty since that first day.

"Something like that," I tell him.

"You can't be kicking me and Poppy out every day," Wells adds as he tosses his pieces into the cut pile.

The ax swings, finds its target, and then I swing

again. I throw my whole body behind it, working the tension out of my muscles.

"You guys don't have to leave. Never minded a bit of voyeurism."

"Hey." Rhett stops and points a stern finger in my direction. "Knock it off."

I hold my hands up in mock surrender. "Wouldn't dream of corrupting young Poppy."

"She's not that young," he grinds out.

"Keep it up," Wells sings as he grabs another beer out of the cooler. "If I were you, I wouldn't push him while he's swinging an ax. Imagine his hands just happen to slip…"

I clutch my chest. "Big brother would never."

"Big brother just might," Rhett mumbles.

"Anyway, it's Saturday, so I think we should go to River's bar."

"I thought you said the truce only extended to the rescue barn while she was with Betty?" Wells asks.

Rhett continues to chop wood in the background like we don't exist. Probably because he's trying to think of a reason he and Poppy have to stay home tonight. I don't think they've joined us on our weekly outings the past three weekends. He isn't getting away with it tonight. He needs to take his girl out on the town some-times. There will be plenty of time to fool around *after* we've all done some drinkin'.

"That's what she said," I tell him.

"But you're not going to respect that."

"I think that's a strong choice of words. I respect that the truce only goes so far, but that doesn't mean we can't see each other outside of the truce."

"Sure." Wells grins and nods.

"You're coming out tonight," I say, pointing my ax in Rhett's direction. "I need Poppy there to help me butter River up."

"Nice." Rhett scoffs. "Don't use my woman to get in another woman's pants."

"I don't *just* want to get in River's pants."

"There it is," Wells says.

"There what is?" I turn toward him.

"'River's just a friend,' you always said. I knew there was somethin' more there."

"We all did," Rhett adds. "Should've seen the way you looked at her. Like she hung the damn moon."

"No I didn't—"

"Never did understand why you fucked every woman in this town but her." Wells takes a seat on his cutting stump. "Still doesn't make much sense to me."

"Because she friend zoned him," Rhett decides to chime in.

"She did not!" I am outraged.

"Oh, so you did get in her pants, then?" Wells asks.

"No!" I all but shout.

"Then she friend zoned you."

"*I* friend zoned *her*," I inform them both.

"Definitely a case of her feeling too important for him to fuck around with," Rhett tells Wells, acting like I'm not standing right here.

"True," he agrees. "Probably didn't want to 'ruin the friendship.'"

"I will use this ax to cut off those air-quote fingers, Wells."

He snorts.

"For real, Hayes. What went on there?"

"Leave him alone." Rhett swings the ax into his cutting stump, leaving it standing out at a forty-five-degree angle while he grabs another bottle. "He's probably embarrassed. Poor thing."

"Ooh!" Wells laughs. "You think he *tried* to sleep with her but couldn't get it up?"

I'm so done with this conversation that I can feel a twitch develop in my left eye.

"She slept with Kyle Flanders."

"Kyle Flanders?" They both grimace at the same time.

"I fucked up." I drag my hands over my sweaty face. "She tried to tell me there was something between us. She tried. I pushed her away. Right into Kyle Flanders' arms."

"I don't remember hearing about that one..." Wells mumbles into the mouth of his beer.

"You wouldn't. Pretty sure she threatened his balls if he ever told anyone."

"And when she found out you were a prick?" Rhett guesses.

I sigh and sit down, already mentally worn-out from this conversation.

"Figures." He shrugs. "Push her away and then get pissed when she does what you tell her to do."

"You act like you've never done it." I feel like we've all done it. Such a childish thing to do when you're young and jealous and have no clue what the fuck you feel for your best friend.

"Of course I have," Rhett says.

"Same." Wells tips his bottle into the air.

"Always figured something along those lines happened. Mixing friends and feelings and sex and all that shit just never works."

"It sometimes works…" I want to believe it can work. If it can't, then I've lost River forever because I can't look at that woman without wanting to hold her.

"How much groveling do you have to do?" Wells asks. "Was it a little tiff? Or like a big-ass blowout?"

"Big-ass blowout." I groan, and my shoulders sag. I was the douchiest of douches. I screamed at her, called her names that no one should ever call a friend. God, if only I could go back in time and kick the ever-loving shit out of my younger self.

Had anyone else spoken to River the way I did, I would've made sure they wouldn't have walked for a week. So I honestly would've deserved it. Probably still do.

"I look forward to watchin' you grovel." Rhett grins in my direction.

"Same."

"Yeah, I bet y'all are."

"Can't wait to watch you try every day. I'm not leaving you guys alone for a second." Wells laughs when I flip him off.

"I'll get nightly recaps from Poppy."

"Glad I can be the entertainment for the rest of the summer."

Rhett's phone goes off, and he tugs the thing out of his pocket.

"Ah, hell." He tosses the rest of his beer back. "Calf's out in the southern field."

"Ooh, a runner?" I ask, ready for a bit of excitement around here.

"Yep. Let's go," Rhett says.

Wells throws his head back with a dramatic groan.

"So much for takin' the rest of the afternoon off."

"I thought I was the one that was supposed to hate this job?" I ask, patting him hard on the back.

"I don't hate the job." He adjusts the hat on his head. "Just not looking forward to how this beer is gonna sit gettin' tossed around by a damn horse."

"Well, if you gotta vomit, do so downwind. Will ya, little brother?"

He laughs sarcastically and swings up onto his horse.

"I'm in charge of how much alone time y'all get in that barn, *big brother*. Might wanna keep that in mind when you're mouthing off," he tosses over his shoulder. I try to flip him off, but he's already riding full speed after Rhett.

"Let's go, Chip," I say, working my horse into a gallop. "We have a calf to wrangle."

CHAPTER SIX

River

HAVE you ever seen a man on horseback rope a rogue calf? Because it is quite the sight. His thighs support his weight on the horse while it gallops at full speed. One hand is wrapped in the reins while the other circles the rope above his head. His hat flies off in the wind, letting his dirty-blond locks whip around his face.

And then, when he throws that lasso out and it gets that calf on the first try, you can't help but succumb to the excitement. At least, that's what's happening to me right now as I watch Hayes' strong arm rope that runaway calf. His muscles bulge, and his smile spreads across his entire face as he shouts into the sky.

Poppy is swinging her fist in the air as she cheers them on. She loses her balance in the stirrups and falls back to her butt. For just learning how to ride, she's pretty confident in the saddle, and I smile big at her when she turns toward me for a second, eyes bright.

I can't let myself get that caught up, but my thighs tense around the saddle of my horse when Hayes turns around to see us both sitting there watching them. The moment we had heard there was a runner, Poppy had urged me to come with her to watch them. She loves seeing her man in action, and I don't hate watching Hayes in the midst of it either.

He tips his hat in our direction, eliciting an eye roll from me.

"They're all stupidly good-looking," Poppy says, still looking at me from where she sits on her horse.

"Must be something in the water on this ranch."

She laughs. "Think it can still have effects on adults?"

"Lord, if it does, I might just move here."

"You don't need it." She rolls her eyes.

"Neither do you." I raise an eyebrow in her direction. She's gorgeous. Poppy needs zero help in the looks or personality department. Me, on the other hand? I'd do anything to change some of these tattoos. And my taste in men.

"Hey, pretty ladies!" Hayes shouts.

God, he is painfully beautiful. There is nothing sexier than a strong man on a strong horse doing cowboy things. Has he always looked this good? I mean, I've had a crush on him since I was eight. But this Hayes isn't a boy any longer. He's got a few days' worth of five-o'clock shadow, and the muscles he's sporting these days are those of a man.

I'm a little breathless.

"What brings you all the way out here, darlin'?"

And a little weak in the knees.

"Poppy thought it would be fun to watch y'all try to wrangle in that calf," I tell him as he hands off the roped calf to Rhett. It's young enough to walk like a dog back to the field it came from. At that age, they're playful but easily led. "Figured one of you would fall and make an idiot of yourself. I was hopin' it'd be you."

Wells snorts so loudly that I struggle to keep my own laughter contained.

"That's not a very nice thing to hope about someone, River." Hayes' grin is playful.

I shrug. "It'd be funny, though. And that's what counts."

"Thought you'd be workin'?" He ignores my jab and walks his horse up next to mine. Poppy has jumped off her horse and walked it over closer to Rhett and the calf. I can hear her cooing at the little creature from here.

"Speaking of," I say, glancing at my watch. "It's time for me to head that way."

"Let me walk back with you."

"I'm not walking."

"Funny." He grins.

"You weren't there to help me with Betty the last few days." I turn my horse back in the direction of the rescue barn where I parked, and Hayes follows suit.

"Rhett's not been too easy to slip free of. And I had to help chop wood today," he says. "No getting out of shit like that when Rhett *and* Wells are involved. So, you're workin' at the bar tonight?"

"Same as every Saturday." My voice is laced with mock excitement. Working at a bar, a restaurant, or retail, you never get a weekend off. But I need the extra money, and in a small town, the tips are actually really good.

"I'll be there tonight."

"Lovely. Have fun."

"You could save me a dance," he says.

"I'll be working, Hayes. And this little truce we have only exists in that barn." I point in the direction of the big barn, where Betty is probably taking her late-afternoon nap. And I realize as the words leave my mouth that this little conversation we've fallen into feels too comfortable. I've let my guard down around him, and it's only been a few days. If I'm caving this soon, what's it going to look like a week from now?

I roll my shoulders back and try to build the walls back up.

"Oh, come on," he says, reaching across the gap in our horses to nudge my arm. "Bill isn't gonna care if you take a three-minute dance break."

"The patrons might."

"It's not like you'd be working alone. Someone else can pick up the slack for a few minutes."

"I hate dancing."

He laughs out loud, throwing his head back and making a show of slapping his knee.

"River, that's a lie, and we both know it. You used to let me swing you around on a dance floor all damn night."

"That was before I got old. Back then, if you were to drop me, I'd just brush it off and keep going. Nowadays, if you dropped me, I'd be limping the next day."

Getting old sucks. I swear, once I turned twenty-eight, it started going downhill. Having a few drinks never hurt so damn bad, and any strenuous physical activity makes me sore the next day. Hell, I'll probably be feeling this horse between my legs tomorrow morning.

And the way Hayes and I used to dance isn't the normal line dancin'. He'd swing me around and flip me over. We were the center of attention of every late-night barn dance we could find as teenagers. They'd cheer us on, and we'd pretend like we hadn't been practicing every chance we got.

But I haven't danced like that in years. There's no way in hell you'd see me being swung around that dance floor anymore.

"I wouldn't drop you, darlin'." His voice sends

goose bumps over my arms. "When have I ever dropped you?"

When I told you I loved you.

"Not happening." I've gotta get out of here. Emotions are trying hard to surface, no matter how much I try to build that damn wall.

I throw my leg over and hop down before tying my horse off. Hayes does the same, fumbling with the reins as he tries to keep up with me. I'm speed walking back to my Jeep when he catches up and grabs my arm. So close. My hand was on the damn car door.

"You run away a lot," he murmurs. "I wish you'd stop doin' that. Give a man a chance to think."

"Think faster."

He chuckles.

"Yes, ma'am." I freeze when his hand goes to my hair. It's braided over one shoulder, and he pushes some stray layers back behind my ear. "Now, tell me you'll dance with me."

"No." I swallow.

"Dance with me, Riv."

"Hayes," I warn. "Stop."

"Dance with me." He's begging, and my walls are crumbling.

The thought of his hands all over my body… I won't survive it.

"Dance with me," he begs again. "Please, River. I won't drop you, darlin'."

Promises, promises.

I sigh and take a step back, getting some air. I can't think straight when all I can see and smell is him.

"Ask me again later," I tell him.

"That's not a no."

"It's not a yes." I bite back a grin as I hop into the Jeep. He shuts the door behind me and leans on the window frame.

"But it's not a no." He's smiling like an idiot, transforming him back into that teenager I knew so many years ago. I can't help but smile back as I roll my eyes.

"See you, Hayes."

"Mhm," he hums as he slaps my car door a couple of times. I turn the engine over and put it in reverse. As I'm backing out, he stands there and watches me, his arms crossed and a big-ass smile on his face.

"That's not a no!" he shouts.

I am so fucked.

CHAPTER SEVEN

Hayes

"AM I being dragged on this adventure just to help you win brownie points with River?"

I look back in the rearview mirror at Poppy, tucked tightly into Rhett's side.

"Dragged." I scoff. "You know you love goin' dancing with us."

"Yeah, city slicker. Don't act like we're dragging you to Sunday school or somethin'," Wells says as he flips through the stations.

I know why she wasn't gung ho to tag along tonight. She and Rhett only get so much alone time, but she's right. I do need her to help bridge the gap between me and River. It's easier to be in her presence when there's a middleman.

"I do make a pretty good wingwoman." She winks at me in the mirror, but I catch Rhett rolling his eyes.

He's not happy about being dragged out tonight either, but where Poppy goes, he follows.

"It's good for y'all to get out once in a while anyway," I tell them. "Get to know the people, and show everyone that Rhett isn't as scary as he looks."

"Feeling very much like the odd man out tonight," Wells says as I park the truck and we all jump out.

"Ooh!" Poppy claps her hands. "I could play wing-woman for both of you!"

"I'm only sharing you *after* I've secured the dance I've come for." I point and boop her nose. Rhett slaps at my hand.

"You sure you remember how?" Wells asks. "I don't think I've seen you fling a woman around since River."

"That's because only River gets to dance with me like that. We're partners."

"Were," Rhett adds.

"What are you guys talking about? Swinging around?" Poppy asks.

"You ever see those men throwin' their dance partners around in flips and between their legs and shit?" Rhett asks her.

"No way!" Poppy turns her big, excited eyes back toward me. "You and River can dance like that?"

"Used to be able to anyway."

"Don't be so pessimistic." She gives Rhett a slap on the bicep. "I'm sure it's like riding a bike."

"Well." I shrug. "Guess we'll find out."

I open the door for everyone, and we file in. The chatter and music are loud, filling the big space so we have to shout to each other. Shit, it's busy. This might hinder my plan a bit. If it's too busy for her to step away from the bar, I'm going to have to switch it up, come up with something new to get River's attention.

"No you don't!" I say, grabbing Poppy's arm with a gentle tug. Rhett was pulling her through the bar to try and find a table, but I want her at the bar with me. He turns around and gives me a not-so-nice stare.

"Hands, Hayes."

"Yeah, yeah," I say, holding my hands up. "I know. I'll bring her back. Please let me borrow your other half for a few minutes."

He looks like he wants to fight me on it, but Wells steers him into the crowd and away from us. Throwing my arm around her shoulder, I steer us straight toward River. She's chatting with some people on our side of the bar, and god damn if her smile doesn't almost stop me in my tracks.

It's been so long since I've let myself see her. I knew she was back but avoided her like the plague for the longest time. Until I just couldn't anymore. But now that I'm looking, I can't look away. That smile lights up her whole face, making those pretty, blue eyes sparkle.

She's kept her hair the same, that one long braid over the side of one shoulder, but she's changed into a black dress and a denim jacket. When she climbs up on the little stepladder because she can't reach the top-shelf liquor, I can see that dress is tight as hell. It's showing off every single curve she has. It'll be perfect for when I'm spinnin' her around on the dance floor.

"Every man in this bar is looking at her ass right now," Poppy says into my ear.

Don't like that. Not one bit.

We find a hole in the people at the bar, and we both try to get River's attention. She waves at Poppy and smiles but throws an annoyed look in my direction. I love how she saves all the special looks for me.

"She looks very happy to see you." I like Poppy. She's always telling it like it is and giving all of our shit right back to us…perfect for Rhett and his grumpy ass.

"I tend to have that effect on people."

"Hey there, friend. What can I get you?" River almost has to shout across the width of the bar, and her gaze is fully directed onto Poppy. She doesn't spare me a glance.

"Hi!" Poppy shouts back. "Beer for Wells and Rhett. And I'll have a rum and Coke — dark rum, please."

"On it!" She spins around, walking off before I can butt in and ask her for what I want.

I turn toward Poppy, open-mouthed and gesturing between all three of us.

"What was that?" I ask her. "You're supposed to be my wingwoman!"

"Yeah, yeah, yeah. I know. I just — wow. I didn't

think she'd completely *ignore* you." She watches River make the drinks. "You have a lot of work ahead of you, I think."

I groan and drop my head back in defeat.

"Did you know—" River says, coming back to stand in front of us. She sets three drinks in front of Poppy and pushes them toward her. But there's a fourth in her right hand. "—that Hayes wants me to dance with him tonight?"

River's pretty eyes turn on me, and she rests her elbows on the bar while holding the whiskey tumbler toward me.

"Oh, yeah?" Poppy asks as I take the brown liquid from River's fingers. "Think you're gonna do it?"

River's eyes go back to Poppy.

"I think one of us would end up breaking an arm." She shrugs and throws a towel over her shoulder.

"Or it could be really fun, and I could see my friend do something amazing!" Poppy with her optimism. "I have full faith in Hayes. I don't think he'd drop you. If he does, I'll have Rhett assign him to stall mucking for an entire week."

Poppy's hand smacks me hard in the center of my back just as I take a sip of whiskey. I almost cough it back into the glass but manage to swallow it and regain some composure.

"Wouldn't matter. Won't drop you," I tell her.

"Come on," Poppy begs. "I would love to see it! They really talked up a big game in the truck on the way over."

"Oh, great!" River laughs. "No pressure or anything."

"I'll make you look good, Riv. Don't worry." I wink at her, and despite the eye roll, I don't miss the way her cheeks blush just slightly.

"When's your break?" Poppy asks her, surging on to get that yes.

River glances down at her watch. "Like, fifteen minutes or so."

"Great. Hayes will come get you, and we will all watch the show!"

Come on, baby. Come on. Say yes.

"Fine. But you're not drinking beforehand." She grabs the glass out of my hand and tosses it in the sink behind her.

"Fine," I agree.

"One dance." She says it again like she can't believe she actually said yes.

"Yay!" Poppy shouts, handing the beers to me as she shoos me away from the bar.

"Shouldn't I stay there and keep her talking?" I ask over my shoulder.

"No way! You got what you came for. Don't push your luck, Hayes."

I hesitate, glancing back to the bar. But Poppy is right there, giving me a not-so-playful shove in the direction of Wells and Rhett.

"Fine!" I concede and spend the next fifteen minutes trying not to watch her every move.

CHAPTER EIGHT

River

THIS IS NOT A GOOD IDEA.

Not only because I clearly cannot be trusted to keep Hayes and my feelings at bay, but I haven't danced in years. I'm pretty sure my body is going to give up halfway through the dance, and I'll probably wake up tomorrow with bruises all over.

But I really, really did love dancing with Hayes back when we were younger. The thrill of being thrown around like that by someone you trusted, with everyone's eyes on you as they clap and cheer you on. That shit is addicting.

And I may have worn one of my favorite dresses just because I *knew* I would end up giving in. It's black and tight, and I hope it's going to drive him a little bit crazy. I even remembered to wear some biker shorts under it so everyone in the bar would be spared a look at my panties.

"Trying to escape?"

I jump. He came out of freaking nowhere.

"No," I assure him. "I just want to put my jacket in the back."

"Here," he says, helping me take it off. His eyes roam over the tattoos covering my arms. I had a few before I left, but the majority were done in the city, and I'm absolutely covered in them now. "I'll put it with Poppy. Don't wanna risk you disappearing on me."

He takes my hand, and we slowly move through the crowd of people. I don't know what's going on tonight, but it's far busier than it normally is. I'm actually surprised I'm able to take a break at all.

"I'm so excited!" Poppy shouts across the table as Hayes hands my jacket to her. "Good luck!"

"I might need it!" I tell her, laughing. "I've never danced to these newer songs."

"You think I didn't request one of ours?" Hayes asks, looking at me with a confused face. "Just gotta let him know when we're ready, and he's playing it."

"Any hints you're willing to give there, cowboy?"

"You'll see."

He puts his arm around my shoulders, and we walk out onto the dance floor. He nods in the direction of our DJ and then lets me do a few spins while people slowly clear out of our way. And when the music starts up, I can't help but throw my head back in laughter.

The song he requested? "Save A Horse, Ride A Cowboy."

"Hayes Black!" I shout through my laughter. "Are you kidding me right now?"

"Never." He gives me a tug, spinning me back into his body. "Remember the steps?"

How could I ever forget them? This was a crowd favorite back when we were doing this every weekend in the barn dances. It had just come out, and people thought it was hilarious. Us included. So we made our own little routine and practiced it almost every night.

Falling back into the pattern is, like Poppy said, kind of like riding a bike. My feet just move to the rhythm as we two-step and warm up. I'm transported right back to the summer nights we spent in the middle of a field on his ranch, far enough away that the music wouldn't wake anyone up. We'd spend hours out there, practicing our flips and swings until the sun started coming up.

Hayes' warm hands guide me through the movements as we move in circles around each other, until the song picks up, meaning it's time for the more difficult moves. But he makes it easy, tossing me into the air and sliding me between his legs like I'm light as a feather.

I forgot how confident being in his arms makes me feel. Before I know it, I'm really leaning into it. I can hear people clapping with the beat and cheering us on.

Hayes looks at me like I'm the only woman in the room, and when the rapping part of the song comes on, I step to the side and let him shine.

He sings the entire part like it was made for him. And toward the end, he pulls me in, wrapping his arms tightly around my torso so we're face-to-face. My hands are on his shoulders, and I'm biting back laughter as he throws his head back and shouts in time with the song, "And we made love!"

People scream in the background, and he throws me high in the air, catching me so I'm striking a pose on his shoulders while he spins us around. I fall back, kicking a leg in the air as Hayes catches me just before my head would've smacked the floor. It's our biggest move that always gets people excited. Especially when my feet go over my head, and I land the flip perfectly.

Just as the song ends, I twist a few more times, and then Hayes dips me, placing his cowboy hat on my head as I come back up. The entire bar erupts into applause, and I'm breathless when I stand back up. He holds me close, his smile taking up his entire face. His wild hair is hanging down in his face, and I take the liberty of pushing some of it back.

He turns his head and kisses the palm of my hand. It's quick, so quick that I don't have time to react before he grabs it and raises it high in the air, gesturing for the crowd to clap loudly for me. My face heats, from the embarrassment of being shown off like this or from his kiss, I'm not sure.

"One more," he says as the music continues on, changing into something slower. "Dance one more with me."

"We can't dance like that to this," I tell him, wiping the sweat from my temples.

"Then dance like this." He pulls me closer and tries to sway me back and forth to the music. A strong hand is on my lower back, his fingertips just north of my ass, while his other hand grabs mine and interlaces our fingers.

"Hayes." I take a deep breath to try and clear my head, but all it does is fill my senses with the scent of him.

"River," he says back, mocking my tone. "Just stop fighting me for a minute and dance with me."

"I did that. I danced with you." I try to pull away, but he holds fast. "I need to get back to work. The bar is covered up."

His hand slides up my back, and he tugs the end of my braid.

"Come on, darlin'." Fuck, when he speaks to me like that, I all but melt. "One more dance. Stop runnin' for a second."

"I don't run." I take his hat off my head and place it back on his.

"Good. Extend the truce."

"Hayes, good god. Don't you ever give it up?"

"Nope." He smiles wider. "Let me make it up to you, River. I miss my friend."

There it is. Friend.

We're still swaying to the music, and I lean forward, resting my forehead on his collarbone. I want to give in. I want to be his friend again. But seeing him, being around him, just makes me feel all the things I've tried to forget.

Can I be friends with him and forget all the shit that happened? It's not even that I'm angry with him anymore. I don't think I am anyway. I'm embarrassed. I'm embarrassed that I spilled my guts to this man and he turned me down…to my *face*. And, sure, I'm still not thrilled with how he handled it when I tried to move on. He said some shit that he can't take back…things that still sting when I think about them.

But ultimately, I'm mortified that whatever we had was one-sided, and I was stupid enough to speak it out loud. Every time I look at him, that's all I can see. Him looking at me like he never saw me before, like he was shocked I would even consider him as more than a friend.

I can't do this. I can't.

"I gotta go."

"River, what?" He tries to hold on to me.

"I need some space, Hayes. Please." I look up at him for a minute, begging him with my eyes.

Please, just let me go.

He relents for a second, and I peel my body away from his, dipping back to the table where everyone else is sitting before he can grab ahold of me. Poppy gives me a sad smile when she sees me storming her way and kindly hands my jacket to me before anyone else can say anything.

I glance over my shoulder and see Hayes waiting for me to leave the table before he comes over. Good. He's finally doing as I ask. I just hope he has the good sense to stay away from the bar for the rest of the night.

I need a break from him. I need to breathe.

CHAPTER NINE

River

"IT LOOKED FUN. THE DANCING."

Poppy and I are taking Betty for a walk. It's been a week since the dancing and a solid two weeks of spending time with Betty every day. She's rewarding me by letting me walk her on a leash. It's a pretty amazing feeling.

"It was," I tell her. "That's the problem."

"Why is that a problem?"

"I told you that things happened between us, right?"

She nods, waiting for me to explain.

"I was in love with him." The words just burst out of me.

"Okay, yeah, I kind of assumed that." She smirks over at me.

"Well, okay. I may have told him and…"

"And he didn't respond well?" She moves to stand in front of me while Betty takes a break to sniff around.

"Not at all. I was delusional, I guess? I thought there was something there." I sigh and try not to look at her. " We were best friends, spent every waking moment together. And sometimes even the non-waking hours. I *swear* there was something there. We danced all the time, he sang his songs to me on the back porch, and we took long drives together talking about everything we wanted to do in life. And he *looked* at me, ya know?"

"What did he say? When you told him?"

"Well, he stood there like a fucking idiot for a hot minute." We exchange a look and laugh. "And then he just told me he didn't feel the same way."

"In those words exactly?"

"You're digging for something you're not gonna find," I tell her. "Yes, those words exactly. He didn't feel the same way and would never want to ruin the friendship by going there."

"Ouch."

"Yeah. I was mortified. I think I literally ran away from him that day." I laugh through the pain of rehashing all of this. "Like literally bolted."

"And you just left? Never spoke to him again?"

"No, no. I mean, that's a huge part of what's going on between us because I told him I loved him, and I was more than mortified. I wanted to crawl into a hole and never leave. God, do you know how embarrassing it is to be turned down by your best friend?"

"I can imagine. But I can't imagine running from it for the rest of my life. Unless…something else happened?"

"I was a late bloomer. Like, really late."

"Hey! Same!" She holds her hand up, and we do a stupid high five before we start walking again.

"Please don't judge me. When you said you didn't really have any close friends, it made me realize that I didn't really either. And I'd hate to lose it."

"Girl, I would never," she assures me. "This happened years ago. Spill."

"I was a virgin. I was eighteen, and I was a virgin. Meanwhile, Hayes was out there fucking any girl in town that would let him get near her. I swear to god that guy had more notches in his belt than the belt was long."

"Shocker," Poppy murmurs.

"Anyway, I was young and stupid and determined not to go to college with my V card still intact. Who wants to still be a virgin in college?" We pause and plop down on the grass, giving Betty a break to sunbathe. "Although, looking back, I would've preferred it over the mess I created."

"What did you do?" She looks over at me like I'm about to tell her the juiciest piece of gossip she's ever heard.

"Well, I went out and fucked the first person I could find."

"Okay…? Why's that so bad?"

"It was someone Hayes knew. Not, like, a best friend or anything. But in a town this small, everyone knows everyone. And he did not take it well."

"Why? That was none of his business. One, he turned you down. And two, as a friend, he should've been supportive."

I shrug. "He was pissed. He said some shit that was not okay, and I avoided him like the plague for the rest of the summer. August came, and I moved to the city without saying goodbye."

"Did he even try to talk to you? At all?"

"Nope." I shake my head. "I thought he would. So I hid away in my room all freaking summer. And believe me, if you knew my mom, you'd know that it was miserable for me to do so."

"What a prick."

"He definitely was." I sigh. "You know, I was just as close to Addie as I was to Hayes and the rest of the clan. And when she died, no one told me."

"Oh, River."

She lays her hand on my arm and gives it a squeeze. It does anything but comfort me. The tears threaten to overflow, and I swallow at the pain in my throat. I have to force myself to take a deep breath and keep going.

"My mom called me the day of the funeral, *after* she

got home from it." I sniff and wipe my nose and cheeks. I'm a mess. "By the time I packed my shit and raced here, it was nine o'clock, and Hayes wasn't around. I went straight to the ranch, but he wasn't there.

"I talked to his parents for a while, telling them I didn't know, that no one had told me. I didn't even know how sick she had gotten. And, of course, Katherine and Clyde being the people they are forgave me instantly. Told me there was nothing to apologize for. I helped Katherine clean the kitchen and talked to Wells and Rhett about all the good times we had with Addie."

"And Hayes?" Poppy asks me. "Where was he?"

"Drunk as a skunk in the bar," I tell her on a sigh. "They told me he ran off after the funeral, and both Rhett and Wells had tried to get him home but couldn't."

"Does he know you came?"

"No. You can't tell him. Please don't. I made everyone promise not to tell him."

"No, of course. I wouldn't."

"He wouldn't have wanted me to see him like that."

"So you went? To the bar?" She turns fully toward me, sitting crisscross applesauce as she leans in closer.

I nod. "I thought maybe I could get him to go home. I was ready to throw all that shit that happened behind us. There was no room for anger or hurt feelings when Addie had just died."

"But when I got there," I continue, "he was blackout drunk, Poppy. He was in the worst shape of his life. When I pulled into the parking lot, he was sitting on the sidewalk, hunched over and passed out cold against the wall of the bar. My headlights flashed across him and the pile of vomit he was sitting next to, and my heart just plummeted."

"Oh, my god. There was no one there helping him? He was just left there?" She looks horrified.

"I'm sure he told them all off, and I found out later that they had called his parents, but I texted Wells when I got there and told them I would get him home. So I slapped him around a bit to wake him up and almost fell over a dozen times trying to get him in my Jeep."

"But you said he doesn't know you were there. Was he that drunk? He didn't remember?"

"He thought he was dreaming or hallucinating. That's all I could make out, honestly. That, and him profusely apologizing for everything he said. But it was mostly just garbled English. And when we made it back to the ranch after stopping only twice for vomit, Clyde and Rhett carried him up the stairs while Wells got him set up for a rough night."

"Wow." She leans back on her hands and looks out over the fields. "That's intense as hell, River."

"It's a mess, is what it is."

"Why didn't you hang around the next day? See him and try to work it out?"

"Finals." I shrug and tell her the other half of that truth. "Fear."

"Finals, I understand. Fear? He obviously had, and still has, great love for you. I can't imagine him turning you away the day after his sister's funeral. No matter how bad the blood was between you two."

"No, he wouldn't have. But I was scared. I was still embarrassed, and I didn't think I could face what had gone on between us while *both of us* were mourning the loss of Addie." I groan and lie back in the grass. "It's selfish. I am a selfish asshole. But it was too much!" I shout to the sky. Betty jumps a little but promptly falls back asleep. "It was too fucking much, Poppy."

"Hey." Poppy leans over to look at me. "There was a lot going on, and you were mourning a good friend. Not wanting to hash out whatever had happened between you and Hayes in that moment does not make you selfish. He had a great support system, and while I think he would've loved to see you, I think he would also understand why you left."

I throw my arms over my face, fighting the second onslaught of tears.

"He's going to hate me when he finds out."

"He's a good guy, River." She pulls my arms away from my face. "He won't hate you. And I think maybe it's time you guys try to heal. There's something there, and I think it would be a shame to lose that love.

Whether or not it's as friends or something more. I just think it might be worth working through."

She's right. I know she's right. So I nod because I don't trust my voice. She lies down next to me, and I take a deep, calming breath.

"Thank you," I tell her.

"Anytime." She grabs my hand, and we lie there together, staring at the clouds. Turns out I was the one that needed a friend.

CHAPTER TEN

River

POPPY LEAVES me to walk Betty back by myself. I told her I have plenty of time before my shift, so I can do all of her evening chores. It'll be good for the responsibility to start switching over to me anyway. Betty needs to get used to someone else taking care of her.

Over the past week, Hayes has stopped in a few times, keeping me company while I sit there and play with Betty. She's started to come out of her shell, letting me brush her, teach her how to sit and stay, and play with her toys. The whole time, Hayes just sits there, letting Betty and me get to know each other while Hayes and I get reacquainted as well.

So much has happened in the last decade, and I feel like I'm getting to know a whole new person. He's worked his ass off on this farm, especially during the times Dean had been gone, putting his music to the side to help his brothers. But he did tell me he's played at the bar on a few occasions when he could slip away.

He's always been an amazing guitar player and singer. Growing up, it was his dream to be a country music star. As he got older, he lost some of that dream when he realized how hard it is to actually make it in the music business.

"You know," he told me yesterday while Betty was playing tug-of-war, "I left once."

"Left the ranch?"

"Yeah. When Dean was back and we thought he was straight. Thought I would try to get out and experience the world a little, play my music in some bigger bars."

"What happened?"

"Hated city life," he said with a laugh. "Missed the ranch. I think leaving made me realize just how much this place is a part of me. So while I miss being able to play whenever I want, I don't miss not being able to see the stars."

I understood where he was coming from. While I loved the city and how there was always something to do any time of day or night, something has clicked back into place since I've been home. It's comfortable and safe, and everything moves at a slower pace. My road rage may have gotten a little out of control living in a city where rush hour just so happened to last all day. But being home, I *want* to drive slower. I want to take the doors off my Jeep and let the sun bake my skin on the back roads.

Life is different here in a good way.

As I approach the barn, I can hear Hayes playing the guitar, and I smile. I've gotten used to the comforting sound of an acoustic guitar in the evenings. And I think it helps Betty relax, too.

"Hey!" he greets us, looking up and smiling wide. He sets his guitar to the side, and I can't help but look him over. His face is a little red from the sun today, and his white muscle tee is no longer white. I love it when he wears those cut-up tees, showing off his muscular arms and strong chest. When he bends over and it falls open, giving me a lovely view of his abs…woof.

"You can keep playing," I tell him when I regain a working brain. "Betty likes a little show with her dinner."

He watches me for a second but then picks his guitar back up, playing one of my favorite songs as I get Betty settled in for the night. He starts singing the lyrics, his deep voice filling the barn.

We still haven't talked about how I ran away from him after our dance last weekend. We've both been ignoring it, acting like everything is fine — like we're friends again. But I can feel the tension. There are things both of us aren't saying, and it's hanging over my head like a damn guillotine. I'm just waiting for it to drop.

"Supposed to rain tonight," he says as the song ends. He keeps strumming random chords, playing with different tunes while I finish up with Betty.

"Another thing I missed in the city," I tell him. "The smell of rain. In Bozeman, it just smelled like metal and dirty sidewalks."

He hums his agreement.

"Wanna go muddin' tomorrow if it rains enough?"

That gets me smiling. We used to go mudding together all the time. A few unlucky times, we had to walk home because there was no signal, and the damn four-wheeler was too stuck for either of us to get it out. I think Clyde was ready to kill both of us every time that happened.

"Don't you have work to do?"

"It's Saturday. I can take a few hours off. What about you? You gotta work?" He sets his guitar to the side and gives me his full attention.

"Just in the evening. No weekends off for bartenders."

"Let's go, then. Like old times. It'll be fun."

I glance over at him, and he's just sitting there watching me, waiting for me to say yes. I don't know why it's so hard to say yes to him. Over the past week, we've kind of fallen into this pseudo-friendship. We both know there are things bothering us or things we need to talk about, but we're both too scared to bring them up. So instead, we just pretend that everything is fine, that we're friends again, and we just go on as normal.

"River." I close up Betty's little room and sit down cross-legged next to Hayes. "Tell me what's goin' on up in that pretty head of yours."

I glance down at my watch, and I know we don't have time for a discussion tonight. But Poppy is right — we have to talk about our shit soon, or it's going to eat us alive. Or blow up…again. But I have to be at the bar in an hour, and I smell like the ranch.

"Alright, mudding it is." I turn to face him. "But if you get us stuck, I am *not* going to be the one getting out to push."

He knows that's not what I was thinking about. I can see him visibly hesitate, like he wants to push me on this. But he decides against whatever it is he wanted to say and instead just gives me one of his panty-dropping grins.

"I'd never expect you to get out and push. I'm a gentleman."

"A gentleman?" I scoff. "That must be a new development because I distinctly remember getting told only you knew how to drive the four-wheeler, so of *course* it had to be me that got out and pushed."

"And we got out, if I recall correctly."

"Once," I tell him, flicking his bicep. "And you gunned it so hard that I face-planted headfirst into the mud."

He throws his head back, laughing.

"Oh, shit. Yeah. I forgot about that."

"Not funny."

"Hilarious, actually." He takes his hat off and sets it on his guitar. "You were steamin' mad. You were so hot with anger that the rain just evaporated the second it hit your skin the whole way back."

I shake my head and try not to give him the satisfaction of laughing.

"You're such an ass, Hayes Black."

"What's that? I have a nice ass?"

"Lame joke." I snort.

Our laughter dissipates, and we sit there in silence for a moment, just listening to the cicadas chirping outside. Hayes moves, scooting a little closer to me until I can feel the heat from his skin. That man is gonna need some aloe.

"River." He reaches out and takes my hand in his. The palms are rough from hard work, and I like the way they make me feel small. He runs his thumb over my knuckles. "I missed you."

When I look up and come face-to-face with him, my heart kicks up a gear, and I have to swallow against the panic. This feels too comfortable, too easy. I'm supposed to be keeping my distance and guarding my heart.

So instead of saying what I want to say, I just smile and then peel my hand from his. He tries not to let me go, but when I stand, he's forced to drop my hand.

"I have to go get ready for work." I walk over to the little work bench and grab my things. "See you tomorrow, yeah?"

His mouth opens and closes while he just watches me stand half in and half out of the barn. I guess part of me is waiting for him to make a move, to stop me from running again. I want him to. I really, really want him to.

But that's not Hayes' style.

So, instead, I just leave.

"Good night, Hayes."

CHAPTER ELEVEN

Hayes

GOD DAMMIT THIS WOMAN. All she does is run.

It takes me a second after she disappears from the barn door to get me moving, but I jump to my feet and take off after her. She's practically running back to her car, and I have to shout to get her attention before she slams the door shut.

"River Marie Larson!"

Her head whips around.

"Did you just full fucking name me?" she shouts back as she watches me run after her.

"Yes." I'm out of breath by the time I get to her. Shit, you'd think workin' on a ranch would have me in better shape. "Because you are fucking running again."

"You didn't stop me."

"I am now!" I throw my hands up in the air. "Tell me what's goin' on up there."

"I don't know how to be friends with you!" She sounds frustrated, like she's two seconds away from crying. "I don't know what friendship looks like for us anymore. A lot has happened. A lot of things were said. I don't know how to be Hayes and River again."

Her blue eyes are wild with emotion, and in the setting sun, her freckles come out to play on her olive skin. She's fucking beautiful. I don't know how to tell her that I want whatever she'll give me. Whether it's casual conversation or late nights watching stupid movies. Whether it's just friendship or something more. I want anything and everything.

"You just be yourself, River," I tell her, taking a step closer. "Stop runnin'. Stop hiding from me. Talk to me."

"I can't talk to you!" She gives me a little shove. Cute. I don't even move. "I don't know *how* to talk to you. You said some really hurtful shit, Hayes."

"And you told me we couldn't talk about it. Do you know how badly I've wanted to apologize? To tell you that I've thought about that day every single moment since you walked out of my life? That I've not had a single good night's sleep since you left town?"

"Don't be dramatic."

She wipes a tear from her cheek and refuses to look at me. So I grab her jaw and force her to. Her eyes bounce back and forth between mine while both of her hands grab hold of my wrist.

"Knock it off, Hayes," she growls out.

"You're being stubborn. It's annoying. So I'm going to make you look at me and hear me. I missed you. I missed us. I am sorry for everything I said, River. I never should've called you all those ugly things."

She sniffles, and the tears overflow. Shit, I didn't mean to make her cry.

"Don't cry, darlin'. It kills me to know I treated my best friend so badly. I'm sorry. I'm so sorry, River. Please, forgive me. Let me make it up to you."

"You were so mean," she whispers. "You broke my heart."

I don't know if me yellin' at her broke her heart or if how I reacted when she told me she loved me did. I'm sure both. But I can't take it back. No matter how badly I want to go back in time and shut my motherfucking mouth, I can't.

I was scared. She told me she loved me, and all I could see was me holding her back, being too attached to this ranch. Not being good enough for her. I was eighteen and fucking stupid.

"I know, River. I know." I tug her into my body, holding her tightly against me. She cries into my shoulder, her breaths hot on my chest as she lets out all that hurt. "Let me keep apologizing until you don't hurt anymore. But don't run from me, River. Be my friend. Let me prove to you that I can be a good friend to you again."

We stand in silence for a minute, and I let her

completely soak my shirt through. It's a small price to pay to feel River wrap her arms around me again. I didn't realize how I took all of her touches for granted back then. But now? I savor every little thing.

She takes a deep breath.

"I want to strangle you."

I laugh and run my hands through her soft hair. She smells like the ranch — honeysuckle and hay. I've missed the way she fits in my arms, and I don't want to let her go.

"Kinky."

"Hayes!" She groans and tries to pull away.

"I'm sorry," I say, trying not to laugh anymore. "Here."

I sit down on the grass and tug her down with me, making her straddle my lap.

"What in the world are you doing?"

Placing her hands over my throat, I lie back flat and put my arms out to the sides. I close my eyes.

"Strangle me. You have more leverage if I'm lying down and you can use your body weight against me."

"Are you out of your goddamn mind?"

I peek up at her, and she's looking at me like I'm crazy, but she isn't crying anymore, and there's a hint of a smile on those pretty lips.

"Probably. But if this is what it takes for you to forgive me, it's a damn good way to go out." I clear my throat and adjust under her. "Just don't judge me if I get a little hard."

"Hayes!" she squeals.

"Because I've always been a sucker for a dominant woman."

"Hayes Black."

"Don't judge a man for his kink, River Larson."

"You're an idiot."

"For you."

She sighs and lets go of my throat, sitting her full weight back on my dick. Probably should've thought this through a little better. I'm only a man, after all, with a gorgeous woman on top of him, thighs spread and hair a mess.

"I'm not going to strangle you."

"Disappointing," I tell her. "I was lookin' forward to a little bit of fun."

She sighs like she's irritated, but I see that cute little smile still gracing her mouth. It makes the little wrinkles around the corners of her eyes pop out, and I fucking love it. Pushing up to her feet, she extends a hand.

"Come on, cowboy."

I grab it, and she pulls me up.

"The truce is over," she says, making my stomach drop. What did I do wrong? Was I too forward? Did I say too much?

"Wha—?"

"No more truce," she interrupts. "I want to be friends."

"Friends," I repeat.

"Yes. Friends. What happened is in the past, and I'm tired of actively trying *not* to like you."

"I knew it was difficult to hate me." I give her my best Hayes grin, and she just shakes her head.

"It is, actually. You're a good guy, Hayes." My heart beats faster at her words, and my chest may puff out a little with pride.

"No more runnin'?" I ask.

"No more running. I promise."

"Good." I sigh dramatically and pretend to wipe sweat from my brow. "I was gettin' tired as hell chasing your ass all over the town."

She gives me a playful shove, and we both laugh as she climbs into her Jeep. The windows are rolled down, and I lean onto the frame to get a better look at her. Fuck, she's gorgeous. I don't know how I ever let her get away back then.

It's not happening again.

"Maybe I'll stop out at the bar tonight."

"Oh, yeah?"

"Keep you company. Keep the men from flocking to you like flies on a hog."

"And I'm the hog in this scenario?" She raises an eyebrow.

"Bad analogy. Anyway, don't need all those men drooling over you while you're tryin' to work."

"Actually, that's when I get the best tips. So maybe save your caveman bullshit for someone else." River winks at me, and I feel my cock twitch.

She's right. I do have a caveman attitude when it comes to her. I don't want anyone else looking at what I consider to be mine. And I know she doesn't know it yet, but no matter how long it takes, at the end of all of this, River Larson is *mine*.

"Have a good night, Hayes."

She throws the Jeep into reverse, and I step away to let her pull out of the driveway. I stand there and wave, and even after she's long gone, I just stand there.

I should've realized that it would take more than nice words to make all the damage I caused go away. She needs actions, not words. River needs to see that I am fucking serious when it comes to getting her back. From now on, I'm on my best behavior, showing her that I am dependable — that I've changed.

"You alright, son?"

Pops scares the ever-loving shit out of me.

"Jesus, Pops!" I turn around and see him rocking in the chair on the front porch. How long has he been there?

"Just making sure she didn't break ya."

I walk toward the main house, up the stairs, and plop

down in the rocking chair next to him. He just smiles and looks out toward the setting sun.

"You eavesdropping, old man?"

"Not my fault you kids decided to put on a show right in front of my house."

"We didn't know you were here," I tell him with a groan. "Maybe announce yourself next time."

He just chuckles.

"You gonna be good to her?" he asks, looking over at me. God, he's gotten old in the past few years. It's crazy how your parents are perpetually thirty-five until one day you look over and their hair is grey and their bodies are weaker.

"I'm gonna try, Pops."

"She always has been head over heels for you, kid."

"Would've been nice for a heads-up back then."

"Some things you just need to figure out on your own. Some things," he adds, "can only be learned from making mistakes."

"You think she can ever forgive me?"

"Depends." He shrugs. "How hard can you love her?"

CHAPTER TWELVE

Hayes

IT RAINED cats and dogs last night, and I'm eagerly waiting for River to pull into our driveway. I told her to meet me at the main house — she hasn't been to my side of the property yet, and I don't think I'm ready to have her in my space. I don't trust myself to keep my hands off her.

When she finally pulls up, I bound off the front porch steps like a dog greeting their best friend. I can feel how wild my smile is, but I get River to myself for most of the day, and that has me wanting to do backflips.

"Hey there, boy. Easy," she teases as she jumps out of her Jeep.

She takes my breath away. Dressed in faded jeans, old boots, and a shirt that has more holes than fabric, I don't think she's ever looked more beautiful. All of her hair is tied up in a knot on top of her head, with little pieces flying away around her face. It makes her eyes shine bright against the grey sky.

"Took a ride out there early this mornin'," I tell her, flipping my baseball cap backward so I can get a better look at her. "It's muddy as hell. Ready to get dirty?"

"Born ready."

Without even thinking about it, we fall back into our old selves. She grabs ahold of my shoulders and throws herself onto my back. Ten years ago, I wouldn't have blinked at holding her like this. But now? I can't stop thinking about how her arms are wrapped around my neck and my hands are so close to her inner thighs…

"Giddy up, then, cowboy!" She leans back and smacks my ass, and I'm so shocked that for a second, I just stand there and listen to her laugh her heart out.

"I'm going to get you back for that."

"Sure thing. Let's go!" She squeezes her thighs and urges me on. I carry her over to the side-by-side, but I cannot get my mind off the feeling of those thighs wrapped around my body. Someone needs to tell my cock to settle the fuck down because right now is not the time.

"The one with the netting? Really?" she asks when I set her down.

"Yes." I give her a look and then start unhooking the netting that acts as a door. "It's been a while since I've done this, and I'd prefer to keep you inside the vehicle."

She climbs in, and I don't stop myself from taking a good look at her ass as she does. When she looks up at me, she catches me, but instead of hiding from it, I just shrug and hook her in.

"Were you looking at my ass, Hayes Black?" She's holding back a grin as she watches me.

"It's a nice ass," I tell her, climbing into my side. "Why wouldn't I look at it? Anyway, you have a hole in your jeans."

"I have a lot of holes in my jeans…"

"No, I mean on your ass." I grin over at her. I don't know how she didn't feel it when she was getting dressed. But there's a big ass rip under her left butt cheek. "I got a lovely view of ass cheek when you were climbing in."

"You're lyin'."

"I'm not."

Her face turns about ten different shades of red as the engine turns over, and she tries to discreetly check the underside of her ass like I can't see her. But when she feels it, she groans and drops her head back on the seat. I can't help but laugh.

"Hayes." I glance over at her as we start driving. "This is not funny. I got gas this morning. I have been walking around with my ass out!"

That gets me laughing even harder.

"Can you not feel the air on your ass?"

"No!" She shoves me hard, causing us to swerve.

"At least, I couldn't. Now that I'm aware of it, I can feel the damn hole."

"Careful, woman."

"No more looking." She points a sassy finger in my direction.

"Aye, captain." I give her a mock salute. "You know, Pops saw us last night."

"What do you mean?" She grabs onto the netting as I hit a hill a little harder than I needed to, sending us into the air for a second. "Like when we were fighting?"

I nod. "Scared the shit out of me. He announced himself *after* you left. Said he was just making sure you hadn't done any damage with the strangling."

She laughs. She does that a lot lately, and I soak it up.

"God, that's embarrassing."

"Eh," I say with a shrug. "He's caught me doing worse things."

"Oh, gross. I don't want to know."

"I was a bit wild when I was younger," I tell her, pushing on to tease her. "Didn't really hide it either."

"Your poor parents." She smiles over at me. "I don't even want to know how many girls got caught in your bed. Or how many parents caught you sneaking out of their houses in the middle of the night."

"I was stealthy. Never got caught sneaking in or out." I wink over at her.

"You were out of control. Like a wild animal."

"I was a lone wolf." I howl to the sky. "Untamed and unclaimed."

"Jesus Christ." She groans and rolls her eyes, but I can see that little grin threatening to pop out. "This is why I'm not surprised you haven't settled down in the past decade."

"River." I clutch my chest and look at her with a shocked expression. "I said I was wild when I was younger. What makes you think I haven't changed my ways?"

"You think I didn't see all those women throwing themselves at you at the bar every weekend?" she asks, an eyebrow shooting up. "I was ignoring you, but I wasn't blind, Hayes Black. I'm actually kind of surprised you haven't made your way through all the women in town."

"You ever see me leave with one?" I'm genuinely curious. Was she even paying attention? She says she saw them throwing themselves at me, but she didn't mention how I slipped out of their grasp, too busy wishing River was the one looking at me.

"I guess not? I don't know." She hesitates. "I was honestly too pissed at you to pay that much attention."

"But you were lookin'." I smirk over at her. "I've changed a lot since you left, darlin'. I'm too old for that shit. I'm ready to act my age, find someone to love, ya know?"

She just nods, all serious now.

"What about you? You get close to settlin' down while you were in the big city?"

Please say no. Please say no.

"Not really." Her shoulders lift in a shrug, and her eyes move out to the land zipping past us. "I had a couple boyfriends here and there, but they weren't what I wanted."

"What do you want?" The words are out of my mouth before I can stop them. I want her to say *me*, dammit.

"I think I knew even when I was there that I wanted to be here." Her head leans back on the headrest, and she looks over at me. "I didn't want to be with some finance guy that couldn't be bothered to get his hands dirty."

"You want somethin' a little rough around the edges, Riv?"

"I guess." She laughs softly and keeps looking at me. Just…looking. It makes me self-conscious. What's she looking for? "I guess I'm just hooked on cowboys."

A little spark of hope kicks my pulse up. Maybe there's still a chance that there could be something here. Maybe I didn't fuck everything up all those years ago.

"Holy shit." She whistles. "We're gonna get stuck."

We've pulled up to the field that gets all the runoff from the hills around it and can't drain for shit. We don't do anything with this piece of land, just use it for playtime whenever it rains.

"I take offense to that."

"I know you don't have the skills to get us out of there." She grins and grabs hold of the netting with one hand and her seat belt with the other. "But by all means, cowboy, take us down."

CHAPTER THIRTEEN

River

I KNOW we are going to get stuck. There is no way in hell this man is going to be able to make a mess of this field and then not get stuck. Rhett is gonna be pissed when we walk back and ask for help. But I grin because that's all part of the fun.

Hayes guns it, and we fly down the hill, bouncing with every little hole we run over. Mud splashes around us, soaking my jeans and boots, and we haven't even gotten to the worst part of it. I'm laughing and squealing as Hayes spins us into mud pit after mud pit.

He shifts, pushes the gas pedal to the floor, and then turns us into a tailspin. I'm thrown into the netting to my right as mud flies up the side of the vehicle. I am *drenched* in mud. From my face to my arms to my boots. I am fucking covered, thanks to that little move.

We come to a stop, and I look over at Hayes, who is

laughing his absolute ass off at me. He's laughing so hard that he isn't even making a noise. His face is red, and his hair is thrown all over his features.

And I just stare at him.

"I hate you."

He laughs even harder at me.

"I hope you piss yourself laughing."

He takes a deep breath and wipes the tears from his eyes.

"That shit was funny."

"I hate you."

"You said that already." He's still laughing, but he's calmed down now. He leans across the middle and starts wiping the mud off my face. "You look pretty good all dirtied up, Riv."

"Mhm," I hum, not impressed with his compliments right now.

"You do!"

His smile broadens as he finishes with my face and moves to my neck. My nipples pebble, but I refuse to believe it's from him touching me. It's definitely just because I'm wet and the breeze is cool. He pulls back and sits in his seat, wiping his hands on his pant legs.

"Such an ass." I shake my head and smile. "You knew what you were doing."

"Good thing I insisted on the nets, right?"

I give his shoulder a hard shove, making him laugh again as he gets ready to take off again. But alas, we go nowhere. The tires spin, and mud gets thrown from the wheels behind us. He tries over and over again, turning the steering wheel this way and that, digging us deeper into the trench he created.

"You going to admit defeat anytime soon?" I ask him.

"You drive a shift?" he asks, looking over at me with a determined face.

"Uh, it's been ages. Probably since the last time we did this."

"It's like ridin' a bike." He unbuckles himself and climbs out of the side-by-side. "Come on," he says, patting the driver's seat.

I sigh and climb over the center to sit where we were.

"Seat's a little warm for my liking."

He laughs and helps me move the seat around to where I can reach the pedals.

"Alright, darlin'." God, I love it when he calls me that. "You're gonna turn the wheel this way and pump the gas *slowly* while I push, okay?"

"I've seen it done a hundred times," I tell him, shooing him away. "I know what to do."

"Okay, well, you haven't driven a stick in over a decade, so pardon me if I'm a bit worried you might accidentally throw it in reverse."

"Shut up and go push."

He grabs my head and pulls me toward him, kissing

me on the side of the head before running behind the vehicle. I sit there, staring at where he was standing. He just…kissed me.

He kissed your head.

Still. He put his lips on me. He never did that, even when we were on the best of terms. Sure, he would hold my hand or let me cuddle on the couch during movies. But his mouth steered clear of any part of me. That's definitely a new development that my heart immediately wants my brain to overthink.

"River!" he shouts. "Earth to River!"

"Sorry! Yeah. Ready?"

When he answers, my brain kicks back into gear, giving me the idea of revenge for soaking me with mud a few minutes ago. If I keep the wheel straight and absolutely gun it, this thing isn't going anywhere. It'll just spray mud all over Hayes from where he's pushing on it.

And that's exactly what I do.

He counts me down and then squats to push the vehicle forward. I slip it into gear — he was right, it is like riding a bike — and press that pedal to the floor. When I look back, he's drowning. From his old baseball hat that he looked far too good in to his boots that are digging hard into the ground. He's covered.

When I stop, he pushes off the bumper and puts his hands on his hips. Dirty water is dripping off his face, and I can't help it. I burst out laughing. Climbing out, I walk slowly back to him while he just stares at me, looking very disappointed at the mess I've made.

"Hayes?" I ask, trying hard to stop the laughter.

I take another step, and he grabs me. I scream when he holds me tight to his muddy body. He's laughing now, too, holding me close with one arm while he tries to smear my face with mud with the other. Hair falls out of my bun and gets stuck in my mouth. I'm pushing on him, desperately trying to escape. I can't breathe, I'm laughing too hard, but he doesn't stop.

He loses his footing, and next thing I know, we're both going down. The mud is cold as shit and soaks through my denim quickly. But before I can stand up, he's tugging on me again, pulling me on top of his lap. I'm straddling him when he pushes the hair out of my face.

We've both stopped laughing now, just smiling at each other. I can't breathe now for a whole other reason. He's looking up at me like he wants to kiss me. And, oh shit, his eyes dip to my mouth and then back to my eyes. I can feel his breath against my cold skin. He's so close.

My hands rest on his shoulders, and his move to my ass. His fingers dip into the hole below my ass and tug me closer. Fuck, he's hard. I can feel his thick length against the seam of my jeans. My eyes dart down to his lips, and that's all the permission he needs.

He kisses me hard, our mouths instantly opening to

one another. My hands run through his hair, knocking the baseball cap into the mud. I've dreamed of this moment my entire life, and it surpasses anything I could've ever dreamed of. His lips are soft, and his tongue explores my mouth like he can't get enough of my taste.

"Fuck, you taste good," he murmurs against my lips, his hands moving to pull my hair out of its knot. His fingers tangle in the unkempt waves, tugging hard to make my head fall back. And then he's kissing my neck. It's covered in mud, but that doesn't stop him.

He devours me.

My heart is threatening to jump right out of my chest, and I can't catch my breath. I'm panicking. While I want to stay in this sexy little bubble with him, I'm terrified of what this is going to do to us. We just decided to be friends last night, and now we're all over each other.

I refuse to be just another notch in his bedpost.

"Hayes," I whimper as he bites the soft spot below my ear. "Hayes, wait."

He stops and pulls away, his hands still twisted in my hair as he looks me over. He looks so concerned, like he's hurt me.

"What are we doing?" I sound breathless.

"I'm kissing you." He kisses me again, and I melt into him again, just for a second.

"We can't." I push a little on his chest, and he lets

me get some room, but his hands are still on me, making sure I don't run away. "We can't do this."

I lick my swollen lips, and it pulls his eyes back down.

"But I like kissing you."

"We're friends."

"Friends kiss."

I laugh and put a little more distance between us.

"I don't want to be that type of friend to you. We just agreed to get back to normal, back to the old us. I don't want to ruin it with this," I tell him, gesturing between our bodies.

He sighs and drops his forehead to mine.

"Can I have one more for the road?"

I grab his face and laugh. "Absolutely not."

"Fine," he groans, giving the side of my ass a quick slap. "Get up, then, *friend*."

That was the hardest thing I've ever done. I could've easily fucked him right here in the dirt, and I'm sure it would've been some of the best sex of my life. But I would've regretted the hell out of it once we were done. I don't want him to fuck me just because I'm around — just because I'm the girl that's giving him a chase.

"You gonna turn the wheel this time?" He's trying to joke, but I can tell I sort of ruined the playful mood. Nothing will cool you off quicker than being told you're just a friend.

I should know.

"We can try, but I'm tellin' you this thing is stuck. We're going to have to ask Rhett or someone for help."

"I'd rather lose my left nut than ask Rhett for help and face his wrath."

I snort.

"Drama queen," I mumble to myself. "Let's try again, then!"

CHAPTER FOURTEEN

Hayes

SO, she was right. Whatever. That thing was so stuck that I got drenched with disgusting field mud over and over again until she put a stop to it, saying I was going to catch my death if we didn't walk back.

I reluctantly gave in.

"Let's go to Wells first," I say as it starts to rain.

"Okay," she says with a shrug. "But he's alone with the dogs today. It's Poppy's day off. He probably won't be able to leave them."

"Shit. So it's either Pops or Rhett."

River shrugs again. "Up to you, cowboy. I plan on making your poor driving skills take the fall for this one."

"That's insulting."

"If the shoe fits."

I watch her for a second as we fall into silence. I'm

kind of surprised we were able to kiss and then just move on like nothing happened. I got worried that once she pulled away, she was going to take off runnin' again. But here she is, smiling and joking. It's making me want to kiss her senseless all over again.

I'm not sure what came over me back there. That's a lie. I've been wanting to kiss River since she came back to town — since I saw her standing at the bar wiping pint glasses. She came back into my life like a hurricane, and I haven't been able to think about anything else since.

When she was laughing, joking around with me like old times, I couldn't stop myself. Her tanned skin covered in mud and her hair sticking out and falling around her face — she looked beautiful. Perfect. I couldn't help but pull her close and lay one on her. And when she kissed me back? Shit. I was a goner.

And so was my dick. He was up and ready to go in 0.5 seconds flat.

"What in the hell happened to you?" Rhett's voice shakes me out of my thoughts as he and Sawyer, one of the ranch hands, approach us from over the hill. Should've known with my luck they'd be out this way.

"Ask your brother," River says, immediately throwing me under the bus.

"I may have gotten the side-by-side stuck."

"That's embarrassing for you," Sawyer says, leaning forward on his horse.

"Par for the course," Rhett grumbles. "Alright, we'll head back and get the truck. Y'all go sit with it. We'll be right back."

"No sense in makin' the lady wait out in the rain," Sawyer adds. "Hop on up, and I'll take you back with us. You can get warm and cleaned up."

Over my dead body is she getting cozied up with another man on a damn horse.

"She—"

"Thanks!" River looks over at me with a smirk. "I'd love that. I am pretty cold."

"Don't you think you should stay with me?" I ask her, an edge to my voice. "Probably should. What-if I start to get hypothermia and I need body heat."

"It is not that cold out." She laughs, and my skin burns when I see her hand slide into Sawyer's.

"Then you'd survive staying out here with me."

Sawyer helps her swing up onto the saddle behind him, and her thighs wrap snugly around his waist. Our eyes meet, and he gives me a smirk that makes my eye twitch as he pulls her arms around him. Rhett just watches it all happen with a knowing look on his face.

Why does everyone suddenly get off on watchin' me suffer?

"You're freezing," Sawyer says over his shoulder. "Let's get you back to the house."

"You can take her to mine!" I try one last attempt at keeping some sort of control of the situation.

River raises an eyebrow at me.

"I've never been to your house."

"So?" I shrug.

I want her to just go with it. Just *go to my house, River.* I want more time alone with her. I want to see if she'll let me kiss her again.

"Just take me to the main house," she tells Sawyer, still giving me a weird look. "My Jeep is there, so I can just head home and get ready for work."

"You don't have to be at work until later tonight. Go to my house. Hang out."

I sound desperate, but the words just keep coming out without my permission.

"Hayes," Rhett barks, interrupting my next word vomit of a sentence that was going to spew out of me. "Go back to the damn side-by-side. It's rainin'. I'm tired of sittin' here watching you beg."

Ouch.

"Fine. But if I get hypothermia or somethin', I want it known that it was River's fault."

"I'll make sure it's in the obituary," Rhett tells me.

Feeling like a scolded child, I turn on my heel and make my way back to the stuck vehicle, River's teasing face stuck in my mind the entire way back.

River

"You sure you don't wanna go inside and dry off?

Have somethin' to drink?" Sawyer asks as I dismount the horse. "I'm sure Katherine has something in that kitchen."

"I'm sure she does," I say with a laugh. "But I'm good."

He's handsome, dark eyes and dark hair, a tan that proves he's out in the sun every day of his life. And those muscles are toned from hard labor. But even with him putting on his best smile for me, I can't stop thinking about the way Hayes kissed me back in the field. He made me feel like I was the center of his world, and I don't think I could get that from anyone else.

"See you around, then, River. Maybe at the bar sometime."

"Yeah, maybe." I give him another polite smile and then slip away to the comfort of my Jeep. I should be interested in him. I should want the sweet looks and compliments. I really should try with someone who *isn't* Hayes.

Instead, I just climb into my Jeep and give him a little wave, signaling he can head back out to help them get Hayes unstuck from the field. I start it up and turn the heat on. To be this cool in summer is a crime, but when you combine rain with the wind coming off the mountains, it's downright frigid. And I do kind of feel bad for leaving Hayes out there by himself.

But I was too busy loving Hayes' reaction to the way Sawyer touched me.

A knock on my window brings me out of my thoughts, and I roll the window down to let Sawyer lean on the frame.

"Somethin' going on between you and Hayes?" he asks.

"Uh, n-no." I can feel my cheeks heat. "No, we're just friends."

"Oh, okay. I just thought he was acting some sort of way, but I could've been seeing things. But this is a good thing."

"Yeah?"

He smiles, his dark eyes lighting up just a bit.

"Yeah. Because now I can ask you out. I know I may have been a bit too subtle earlier. Blame it on being a little shy."

"You?" I ask him, struggling to believe anyone that looks like him could be shy.

"Go out with me?"

My brain and my heart are at war right now. My heart is screaming that Hayes kissed me, and that means something. It doesn't want me to abandon whatever it is that's happening there or ruin it by going out with someone else.

But my brain is all logic, telling me that Hayes threw my love back in my face all those years ago and that the kiss means nothing. I mean, how many people over the years has Hayes kissed anyway? Too many to count, I'm sure. It probably meant absolutely nothing to him.

It was just the moment getting the best of him. We're just friends.

So in the end, my brain wins because it puts up a far better argument.

"Um, sure." My stomach flips as the words come out. I immediately regret it. But Hayes and I are friends now. I have to get past this stupid crush I have on him, or I'll never meet someone.

"Don't sound so excited." He grins, his eyes playful.

"Sorry, you just caught me off guard. I mean, look at me." I gesture to my body and how I'm covered from head to toe in mud. "I don't think I look super appealing right now."

"Then you have no idea how beautiful you are." His voice is smooth and buttery, and I try to tell my heart just to give him a chance. It's just one date. Hell, maybe I'll end up liking him.

"Okay, lover boy. Calm down." I laugh.

"Next weekend? Let me take you to dinner before your shift."

I take a breath. I can do this. I can totally do this. I am available. That kiss with Hayes meant nothing.

"Yeah. Let's do it." I put on my brightest smile. "I

just have to be at work by seven, so it'll have to be an early one."

"Fine by me." He leans back and taps the top of the car. "See you then, River."

I give him a little salute and then roll the window up. Not waiting for him to get back up on the horse and leave, I back out and gun it down the driveway. I have to get off this ranch before I run back and cancel the plans. Forcing myself to go on this date will be good. I need to get out more.

Although, I can't help but wonder what Hayes' reaction will be when he hears about this…

CHAPTER FIFTEEN

Hayes

I SPENT all weekend trying *not* to text River too much. After what happened on Saturday, I figured I should give her some space. But that's a lot more difficult in practice than in theory.

"You comin' to see River today?" Wells asks as we sit at the old dining room table in the main house. Momma cooked us all a huge breakfast, and we've been sittin' here shooting the shit while ranch hands wander in and out.

Mondays are slow.

"Planned on it." I lean back in the rickety chair. "Got some people headin' in today to rent out some stalls for their barrel racers. Their barn is being upgraded, so they need a place to stay while that's being done. After that, I'll head over for a bit."

"How's that sweet dog doin'?" Pops asks.

"Making a lot of progress," Wells tells him with a smile. "Between Hayes, Poppy, and River, they've got her playing outside and going on walks every day. She's not jumpin' at every little noise anymore either."

"Crazy what love'll do to ya." Pops' eyes slide over to me for the briefest second, but I catch it. And so does Wells. An ornery smile comes across his mouth. I don't like it.

"Pops, did you hear about Sawyer askin' River out on a date?"

My blood runs cold. I can physically feel all of the blood rush out of my head, leaving me dizzy.

Pops glances at me and then back to Wells, but I'm frozen, staring at the table in front of me.

"Didn't hear that," Pops finally says, breaking the silence. "Good man, that Sawyer. He's been with us a long time."

"You feeling alright, Hayes?"

My eyes shoot up to where Wells is sitting across the table. I'm going to punch that smirk off his face. I am. There's no stopping me. Once I get him alone, I am going to absolutely smack the shit out of him.

"Fine." I smile. "Why wouldn't I be fine?"

"No reason." He's still grinning. "You just started lookin' like shit."

"Language," Momma whispers as she walks into the kitchen. Wade and Jo are behind her, talkin' a mile a minute about something fun they did with Poppy over the weekend.

"Hey, everyone! Look at my *lightsaber*!" Wade shouts to the heavens. He jumps in front of Jo, cutting her off midsentence as he thrusts the glowing green toy into the air. He's quite the sight, still dressed in his pj's with a chocolate milk mustache.

"That was rude," Jo mumbles, walking around him to join us at the table.

"That's super cool, bud," Pops tells him as they start inspecting the thing together.

"Hey, Uncle Hayes." Jo sidles up to me. "Why do you look so sad?"

"Someone pissed in his Cheerios."

Her eyes shoot to her Uncle Wells, who is trying his hardest to not laugh at her shocked expression.

"Y'all have bad manners."

"Yes, they do," Momma agrees as she attacks Wade's dirty mouth with a wet cloth.

"Did something happen with River?" Jolene's attention is back on me.

The kitchen was full of noise a second ago, but now the only sound is Wade's toy as everyone goes silent, waiting for my response.

"Why would you ask that?" I ask her.

"I heard Poppy and Daddy talkin' about how you're head over heels for her. And I think that means you *like* like her. Like Daddy likes Poppy." Her little shoulders lift up in a shrug. "Just thought maybe River doesn't *like* like you, and you were sad about it."

Great. Good to know I'm the subject of my brother's pillow talk.

"She's goin' out on a date with Sawyer." Wells jumps into the conversation before I can even give her an answer.

"I am not sad." My eyes cut to him and then back to Jo. "I'm just a little tired, is all. And there is nothin' going on between me and River, okay, string bean?"

"But that's not what Poppy says…"

"Poppy is—"

"Watch it," Rhett growls.

I roll my eyes. "Poppy is just mistaken. River and I are friends."

"Hey." Momma claps her hands to get everyone's attention. "I saw that our blackberry bushes are over-flowin'. How about we go pick a bushel and make some pie?"

"Can I bring my lightsaber?" Wade asks at the same time Jo starts to bounce up and down, shouting her excitement.

"Lightsabers are welcome to come along, yes. But they will not be used to hit your sister, correct?"

"Correct," he says.

I'm on edge all morning, just waiting until it's time to go meet River. It takes entirely too long to deal with the renters. Between showing them around and having to unload all five of their horses, it's hours before I'm done and they're driving away. One quick glance at my watch, and it's already after three. I'll be lucky if River is even still here.

And I have to walk over because by the time I get Chip out and tacked up, I could have already been there. So I speed walk — practically jog — over to the rescue barn that's on the other side of the field, running lines the entire way. Like what I'm going to say to her and whether or not I should point out that I know about her date with Sawyer.

I don't like it. At all. After that kiss this weekend, I thought maybe we would be headin' toward something, but she's really taking this friends thing to heart. Is she going out with someone else just to push my buttons? Does she know it's going to push my buttons? Surely, she does. She saw the way I reacted to him flirting with her on Saturday. She has to know.

And I *kissed* her. Doesn't that mean anything?

"You're late today," Poppy says when she sees me walking up to the barn. She's filling up buckets of water for the dog's water bowls. "Horses take longer than you expected?"

"Chatty people." I look past her to see River playing tug-of-war with Betty and take the opportunity to speak to Poppy outside. "Hey, what's this I hear about you and Rhett sayin' there's something going on between me and River?"

I smile when she bites her lip and tries her hardest not to look guilty. It doesn't work.

"Jolene has good ears," I tell her, lowering my voice so River doesn't hear.

"God, sometimes I forget just how nosey kids can be." She gives me a sympathetic smile. "Sorry about that."

"You know anything about this date she's going on?" I nod back toward River.

Poppy pretends to zip her lips.

"I cannot be the go-between," she says. "If I start telling you what she tells me and vice versa, neither one of you will want to be my friend. No one wants a friend that spills the beans."

"Fine," I groan. "Can you at least give me a hint? Is she excited? What's she wearing? Where is he takin' her?"

"I'm. Not. Telling. You."

"You harassing her for secrets?" I look up at River's voice to find her staring at us while playing with Betty. "Because she's a vault."

"A vault," Poppy agrees.

"I don't know what you're talkin' about, Larson." I try to shrug nonchalantly and grab the full buckets for Poppy. Why am I calling her by her last name? I never do that. Fuck, I feel awkward. "I was just makin' conversation."

"Sure you were." Betty notices me and slowly walks over to receive her cautious pets from me before going back with River.

"What would I even be asking her about?"

"Okay, I'll be back!" Poppy calls out and waves. "Give you two some privacy."

"We don't need privacy!" River calls after her, but it's too late. She's off.

"What would I have been asking her about, River?"

She turns back toward me and smiles.

"My date," she says, smiling down at our feet. She won't look at me.

"Hadn't heard. Who with?"

This is killing me inside.

"Sawyer." She looks up at me with those big blue eyes and cheeks tinged pink with embarrassment. "He asked me on Saturday after he brought me back. Figured it couldn't hurt. I need to get out more anyway."

"Kiss me and then run off with another man on the same day. Ouch. Talk about a blow to my pride, darlin'."

"Hayes." She laughs. "We've gone over this. We're friends."

She gives me a little shove in the center of my chest, right where this hurts the most. I grab her hand and give her a tug. The laughter disappears from her face when I won't let her get away.

"What-if I don't want to be just friends with you, River?" What the fuck has come over me? Why am I doing this right now? I plead insanity. River makes me fucking insane.

Her eyes start to water.

"I'd say that's a cruel fucking joke to be playing." She pulls her arm from my grip. "And that you should remember how long it took us to get back to each other this time because I don't think we'd make it back again."

"I'm sorry." I take a step back, wishing I could have a do-over. I want to rewind the last ten minutes and unsay everything that just came out of my stupid mouth. "I'm sorry, River. You're right. It's been a long day, and while that's no excuse, I'm just fucking tired."

"It's fine." She clears her throat, clearly trying not to cry. But now it's just awkward, and I hate myself for making her feel like shit. She was excited before I got here.

"It's not. I'm gonna go."

"You don't have to go, Hayes."

"No, I know." I try to smile. "I'm fine. Like I said,

tired."

"Will I see you tomorrow? I was going to teach Betty some new tricks." She reaches out and tries to touch my forearm, but I step back again. If she touches me right now, I'll lose what little restraint I have. "Could use your help."

"Um, maybe. Yeah, I'm not sure when I'll be able to make it back here. Busy week." Lies. Lies, lies, lies. I try to laugh a bit and smile. I don't want her to think I'm avoiding her, even though that's exactly what I'm doing.

Because I don't think I'm ready to see her be excited about another guy.

"Oh, okay." She's disappointed. *Fuck*. "That's fine. I understand. I'll see you around, then."

She sits down and starts petting Betty, and I stand there for a second, feeling incredibly awkward before finally just leaving. I don't say another word; I just leave her there, sitting on the barn floor, almost crying.

"Hey! That was fast!" Poppy is sitting on the front porch of the main house, sippin' on some of Momma's sweet tea. Her smile drops when she sees my face. "What happened?"

"Not right now. Please, Poppy."

"Oh, okay," she says softly.

And I just keep walking. Past the main house, out to the old dirt drive that leads to mine, and straight into my kitchen to pour myself the strongest drink I own.

CHAPTER SIXTEEN

River

A FEW DAYS LATER, after no sign of Hayes at the rescue barn, I'm spilling my guts to Evie at work.

"So you tell him about your date, and he gets all weird." Evie shrugs from where she's sitting on the counter. It's a slow day, so we're both just hanging out in the back room until the next appointment. "Just sounds like he's jealous."

"He can't be jealous," I insist. "He's never felt any type of way about me. We're friends."

"He kissed you." She looks at me like I'm stupid.

"It was a heat-of-the-moment thing. We were just having fun, and he was probably just swept up in the excitement of it all."

"But you said you stopped it. Not him."

"Because I knew we should stop before it went any further."

"Did he always act like this when you told him about your dates and stuff? Like when you guys were friends in high school?"

"Well…" I pick at my string cheese while I try to think of how to put this without sounding like I was the world's biggest loser in high school. "I didn't really date."

"You've got to be kidding me," she says, a shocked look on her face. "You're hot. There's no way the boys weren't fawning over you."

"Thanks." I smile over at her. "But I was an awkward teenager. I came from a home without a lot of money, and that meant never dressing with the trends or eating homemade lunches in the cafeteria. There wasn't any room for extracurriculars because we couldn't afford it, so making friends was tough."

"But you had Hayes."

"I had Hayes."

"Since you never dated back then, is this the first time he's been around you dating? Maybe he wants what he can't have. He took you for granted, but now that you're trying with someone else, he realizes what he was missing out on!" She wags her eyebrows playfully.

I don't want to tell her about that one time… The time I told him I had gone on a date that ended with losing my virginity.

"But he told me about his escapades all the time." I

groan. "God, he fucked anything that moved. And I had to sit there and let him talk to me like I was one of his guy friends."

"Hiding your true feelings the entire time. That had to suck."

"But we're friends again. And adults. Isn't that what friends do? Share this kind of thing?"

"Look." Evie hops off the counter and sits next to me at the table. "I cannot claim to be an expert in men, but I can tell you that there's a lot of emotions there. I obviously don't know everything that happened between you both, but I've got the gist from what you've told me.

"And if he kissed you," she continues, "then there's something there. It doesn't matter if he got caught up in the moment or had it planned. Either way, he *wanted* to kiss you, River. That means something."

"I don't want to get tangled up in Hayes all over again." I run my hands over my face and sigh. "I know what he's like. I've never seen that boy settle down with one woman. What-if he just wants me like he wanted all the other women he's been with? I wouldn't be able to just have sex with him and then pretend like everything hasn't changed."

"I know you just moved back recently, but since you've been back, have you seen him with anyone?"

I don't have to think about that because even though

I've been avoiding him like the plague, I still watched him like the sad sack I am.

"No."

"And I can tell you that in the last few years, I've not seen him with anyone either. Maybe he's changed those fuckboy ways from his past." She shrugs and leans back in the chair, looking pretty confident in her assessment. "Just sayin'."

"Mhm," I hum. "Whatever."

Maybe she's right. Maybe Hayes has changed. The thought of that fills me with hope that maybe he does feel something for me? If he does, would he want something more than sex? There's no way I could sleep with him and then go back to being friends. My heart couldn't take it.

God, it's been over ten years, and this all just throws me right back into all of those feelings. You'd think growing up and separating myself from him and this town would mean that I could come back here and live a normal life. It *should* mean that. It should mean that he wouldn't have this stupid nauseating effect on me anymore.

But here we are.

"Where is Sawyer taking you this weekend?"

"No clue," I tell her. "I figure he'll pop by the rescue barn at some point and make plans."

"You didn't give him your number?"

"No." I look at her like she's crazy. "I don't just hand out my number to random people."

"River." She laughs. "He's not some random dude. He works on the ranch, and he asked you out. How do you expect him to get in touch with you?" Now it's her turn to look at me like I'm crazy. Which, I guess I understand, but the thought of a guy having unlimited access to me like that kind of freaks me out. That probably says a lot more about me and my still-present feelings for Hayes than anything else.

"He knows I hang around the ranch. Or if he doesn't, someone else will tell him, and he'll come find me. Get off my back," I tease.

"I expect a full rundown after this date. I want to know if Hayes shows up and throws you over his shoulder like a white knight coming to rescue his lady."

"You are delusional." We both laugh. "Hayes would never. Are you kidding me? Plus, I'm not telling him where we're going."

"Like he couldn't find out. Please. No one in this town can keep a damn secret. And even if they could, Hayes could literally just walk down Main Street and check all the restaurants." She winks at me. "He'd find you if he really wanted to."

"That's creepy as hell. That is, like, stalker behavior."

"It's hot. Have you never read a romance book where the hero gets all possessive and stalkery? Hot as hell." She fans herself and smiles. "What I wouldn't give for a man to love me like that."

"That stuff is only hot in books, Evie." I grin at her dramatics. "Those are walking red flags in real life."

"Po-tay-to, po-tah-to."

She shrugs, and I'm desperate to change the subject.

"Are you dating anyone?"

"Uh, no," she says, her face falling a bit. "I was, but it didn't work out."

"Why not? If you don't mind me asking…"

"No, it's fine. I don't really like to talk about it, but he just couldn't put me first. Had some issues he needed to work through."

"I'm sorry." I reach across the table and give her hand a little squeeze, making her smile in my direction.

We fall into a comfortable silence, eating our snacks and listening to the animals snore quietly in their crates. It's so nice in here when everyone is settled, and there aren't a ton of dogs walking in and out to screw with the ones that are boarding. I wonder if I'll ever be able to bring Betty here with me.

A few of the other girls that work here have dogs and bring them in most days so that they don't have to be alone all day. It would be a great way to get Betty some socialization, and she seems okay with the dogs at the ranch. Maybe I could work her in slowly.

"Alright, I need to go give out the afternoon meds,"

Evie says, getting up and throwing her trash away. "Almost time for you to go home?"

I check the clock on the wall.

"Only fifteen more minutes, and then I'm free."

"If I don't see you again before the weekend, have fun. And I'll pray that Hayes comes to his senses and stakes his claim, carrying you out of that date like a caveman."

I just smile and roll my eyes.

"Okay, Evie. I'll let you know if Hayes loses his goddamn mind."

CHAPTER SEVENTEEN

Hayes

I'VE BEEN AVOIDING River all week. I can't face her. I don't know when I became this person, but I don't like it. It's not like I have any type of claim on her. We are friends. She's made it clear she doesn't want more than that.

"I feel like I've blown it." I'm lying on Rhett's couch, talking to him, Poppy, and Wells while the kids are asleep upstairs. It's late, and we all had dinner together earlier, followed by one too many drinks on my part. "I know I've blown it."

"Blown who, exactly?" Wells snickers.

"Your humor is not appreciated at this time," I tell him.

"I think you should probably communicate a little better," Poppy advises. "Not to be a go-between, but from what I've heard, you haven't even hinted at the fact that you might be interested in more than friendship.”

“I kissed her!”

“Keep it down.” Rhett throws a pillow at my face.

“Did you discuss the kiss?” Poppy asks.

“It’s a kiss. What’s there to discuss?” I sink deeper into the couch. “This woman has me losing my goddamn mind.”

“And as a result, so are we.” Rhett gets up to go to the kitchen, presumably to get another beer. Poppy smiles up at him as he walks past, running her hand over his arm in a small gesture of love.

“That!” I point across the room at them. “See that! I want that.”

“Arm touches?” Poppy asks.

“Arm touches. Little looks.”

“Aww,” Wells coos. “He wants love.”

“You shut your face.” I point at him.

“You’d have to stop sleeping around,” Rhett quips from the kitchen.

“I have.” Kind of annoying that they haven’t noticed. “I haven’t been with someone in like two years.”

I turned twenty-eight, Dean started getting really bad, and Rhett started worrying about the ranch, and everything just kind of hit me. The city life hadn’t been for me, and I started to realize that maybe the lifestyle I had been living wasn’t either. So I stopped dipping my wick every chance I got and started focusing on other things. More important things.

Like building my house and starting a savings account. It started to feel like I was getting too old for living the same way I did when I was nineteen and twenty. If I wanted to have a nice house, a wife, and some kids, I needed to get my shit together.

"I guess I haven't been paying attention," Wells admits. "But now that you mention it, I haven't seen you turning into the driveway on two wheels, late as shit because you were out all night in a long time."

"No women hailing calling cabs from the main house either," Rhett jokes as he sits down and tugs Poppy into his lap.

"I want all the good stuff. Wife, kids, noisy house. Started to realize I wasn't going to get that if I didn't settle my shit down."

"So tell her that." Poppy shrugs like it's the easiest thing in the world.

"I can't just walk up to her and tell her that."

"Why not?"

"Because I would look like a crazy person. And we have history. Not so good history, I might add. She'd think I was insane, or she'd slam the metaphorical door in my face."

"So." She leans forward. "You kissed her but won't talk about it. You want to date her but won't talk about it. You don't want her going on that date with Sawyer, but you won't talk about it. What do you guys talk about?"

"Any of y'all know where he's taking her, by the way?" I ask, ignoring her question.

"Why would we tell you?" Rhett asks.

"What are you going to do with that information, Hayes?" Poppy gives me a look that I don't appreciate.

"Nothing. Just curious."

"On that note, I'm off. Early start tomorrow." Wells stands, and I decide I should probably go, too. Sitting around here drinking all night isn't going to make getting up tomorrow morning any easier.

"I'll walk with you," I tell him. Our houses are in the same general direction anyway.

"If you really like her," Poppy says, her voice low while Wells and Rhett talk about something else, "you need to talk to her about it."

"I'm telling you she doesn't want to hear it, Poppy."

"Yes, she does. Make her listen. Do a grand gesture or something!"

"Stop scheming, woman," Rhett tells her, pulling her into his side.

"I'm not *scheming*," she says. "Just helping your brother."

We say good night, and then it's just me and Wells walking back across the pasture. It's starting to get chilly in the evenings now. After that last big heat wave we had, it's been nothing but mild, sunny days and cool nights. One of the benefits of living near mountains.

"You gonna tell River?" he asks me.

I shrug. "Guess I need to. Scares the shit out of me, though."

"River?" He looks over at me with a confused expression. "That girl is one of the nicest people I know."

"She is, if you haven't fucked her over in the past."

"It seems like you guys are on good enough terms now. She danced with you, and hell, she kissed you back. That's gotta mean something, right?"

I drop my head back and look up at the sky. I hope it means something. I really do. But *fuck*, I'm scared.

"It might."

"I'm not going to tell you what to do here," he says, "but I think you should give it a shot. If you're serious about her. Don't fuck her around again, okay? Because we all watched her fall in love with you over and over again when we were growing up. Hell, even Addie talked about it."

"Yeah? She never said anything to me."

"She did to me. She could see how head over heels River was for you, and she knew there was something there. Addie would tell me all the time that you were just too chickenshit to do something about it."

"Sounds like Addie." I laugh. "Brutally honest."

"Do you think you had feelings for River back then?"

"Probably. Looking back, I cared for her far more than I should have as just a friend. She's always been beautiful and funny and fun to be around."

"You used to cuddle," he says like that's all the evidence a person needs. "You'd have movie nights, and I'd come into your room just to see y'all cuddled up together *in your bed.*"

"It was platonic cuddling."

"Not to her, it wasn't. And I don't think it was to you either. I think you were just too thick-headed to do anything about it. Too caught up in all the other women who were throwing themselves at you."

"Probably." I shove my hands into my pockets. "So, yeah, okay. I liked her. And I was scared that if anything happened, the friendship would be fucked. I was scared that if anything happened, she'd see me in a different light and end up hating me. So I thought staying friends was the best thing for it."

"And yelling at her for sleeping with someone else... Was that out of fear, too?" He raises an eyebrow in my direction.

"Yeah, that was the fuckup to end all other fuckups. But it's not like she's without fault either." I can't help but say it because I've been thinking about it.

"What do you mean?"

"She didn't come to Addie's funeral, Wells." I

glance over at him, but I can't read his face. He's gone silent. "I know that I may have made her feel like she wasn't welcome, and that's on me. But she was friends with Addie. That should override any of our shit we had going on. She should've been here."

"Talk to her about it." His whole demeanor has changed.

"You know something I don't?"

"Just…talk to her about it." We pause because this is where he needs to leave me to go to his own house. He refuses to look at me, though. Something is up, and he won't tell me. "Talk to her about everything, Hayes. You want it to work, you have to communicate."

"Since when did you get so knowledgeable about women and relationships?"

"Always have been." He smiles and pats me on the shoulder.

"You're not tellin' me something…but I'm gonna let it slide because clearly, it's something I need to hear from her."

Wells nods.

"So hear it from her. Talk to her."

"Yeah, yeah, yeah. I'll talk to her. Shit. Y'all are annoying, you know that?"

"What else is family for?"

He walks off toward his own little piece of property that Pops gave him, and I stand there for a second before walking off toward my own. It's late, but I pull my phone out anyway. I know she's sleeping, and I know I shouldn't text her after I've been drinking.

But I do.

> Me: Coming to the ranch tomorrow?

It only takes her a minute to reply.

> River: Can't. Working a lot. I'll be back on Monday.

> Me: Let's talk then, yeah?

It takes her a bit longer this time, but finally, a response comes through when I'm back at my house.

> River: Okay.

I'll take it.

CHAPTER EIGHTEEN

Hayes

OKAY, so, I can't do it. I can't wait until Monday, after she's had her little date. That's just not gonna work for me. So instead, I'm walking around town like a fucking madman hunting for his prey. I pop my head into every restaurant or bar they could be in until I walk past Rudy's and see her pretty black hair.

I duck back out of sight and pace in a circle. This is insane. This is literally the most insane thing I could do. I am out here, basically stalking her, trying to find wherever the hell Sawyer decided to take her.

And I don't mind Sawyer. He's actually a really good worker, and he's been a part of our ranch family for a long time. But that's the reason I came out here. He's good for her, and I don't want her to decide he's better for her than I am.

I sound fucking insane. But I can't let her finish this date without knowing what I want and how I feel. My sanity won't let me. Fuck, but my feet will. I start toward the door, and they stop me, turning my ass back around. Not only do I sound insane, but I look insane. People are walking around me like I've lost my goddamn mind.

Maybe I have. River seems to have that effect on me.

Okay, fuck it. I came all this way into town for a purpose. May as well get this shit over with. Rip it off like a Band-Aid.

"You got this," I whisper to myself, trying to give myself a pep talk. It doesn't really work, but here we go.

I walk past the large window with Rudy's lettering on it and push past the old glass door. The smell of burgers and fries hits me, and the realization of what I'm doing hits full force. I'm walking into a crowded restaurant to tell my woman she's mine. I'm about to interrupt a date between my best friend and a nice guy. Shit, I can't do this.

But then Sawyer looks up and sees me. He shoots me a little smirk and then leans across the table to say something to River. I can audibly hear her say, "What?" and then her angry face whips in my direction.

Fuckfuckfuck.

Too late now. Time to commit.

Before she can make it out of the booth, I'm walking up to their table. God, she looks beautiful. She's let her hair be a little wavy, and her makeup is all done, making her blue eyes shine…with anger. She's madder than a wet settin' hen.

And I'm hard.

"What are you doing here?" she growls out, her mouth barely opening. She's lookin' around like she's terrified I'm about to make a scene.

"Sorry to interrupt," I say to both of them as I slip into the booth next to River, pushing her over a bit as I fight to make room for my tall frame. "But I couldn't let this go on without sayin' my piece."

"Hayes, excuse yourself from my date." River's cheeks are a bright pink. "Or I will shove you out of this seat onto your ass."

"That's a bit rude, don't ya think, darlin'?" I smile over at her and then steal a fry from her plate. "Sorry about this, Sawyer," I say, looking over at him. "But a guy's gotta do what he's gotta do for his woman."

Sawyer grins and leans back in his chair, gesturing for me to continue.

"I am *not* your woman."

"Not yet." I wink at her. "But once I carry your ass outta here, you will be."

"Hayes," she says in a warning tone. "Don't you dare."

"Look, River." I turn toward her, getting serious. "You're my girl. I fucked it up back in high school, and I don't want to fuck it up again."

She sighs and leans her face into her hands.

"Please don't do this here." She's whispering now, and it sounds like she's holding back tears. But it's too late now. I have to keep going.

"Nowhere else for me to do it, darlin'. I couldn't wait any longer. I want you — I *need* you, River."

"You want to fuck me, you mean." Some of that spark is coming back now as her eyes find mine again. She's got some fire in her belly now. "I refuse to be another notch in your bedpost, Hayes Black. I know what you were like back then, jumping from girl to girl and bed to bed. That's not what I want. I'm almost thirty, and I'd like to actually *date* someone."

"You don't know me now. You have no clue what I'm like now. Have you seen me with a single woman since you've been in town?"

"That doesn't mean anything. Maybe you're in a dry spell."

Sawyer chokes on his drink, trying to cover up his laughter. Not a fan of having an audience for this, but I guess that's my own damn fault.

"If I am, it's been a pretty long one." I play with the ends of her hair. "It's been years, River. I got my act together, realized I needed to grow up. And while I may have never realized it back then, I realize it now.

You're mine. I don't want anyone else. Just you, firefly."

Her eyes tear up at the old nickname I had for her when we were little. She used to run barefoot around the ranch in the evenings, catching fireflies in her hands and bringing them to Addie, who couldn't run around. And then they'd both watch them fly away before River went on the hunt for more.

"That's unfair," she says, her voice cracking.

"Never said I fight fair."

"Great timing, Hayes," Sawyer quips from his side of the table, heavy on the sarcasm. He doesn't look too annoyed. If anything, he seems to find it all entertaining.

"Come on," I tell her. "We're going home."

"Excuse me?" She watches me stand and hold out my hand. She just stares at it like I've asked her to run away with me. Which, I kind of have.

"I said, come on. We're going home. And you can either take my hand and excuse yourself from this date. Or..."

"Or?" she asks, her eyes going hard with determination.

"Or I'll throw your ass over my shoulder and carry you out kickin' and screamin'."

"You wouldn't."

"I think he might," Sawyer adds, laughing when she

looks at him with the same shocked expression. "Just go, River. It's fine. He's clearly head over heels."

"No!" she cries out, throwing her hands in the air. "Y'all have both lost your damn minds. No. I'm going to finish my date with Sawyer," she says, lookin' at him. "And then we will talk on Monday."

River crosses her arms and looks at me. I can see the dare in her eyes.

Sawyer and I exchange a look. He shrugs his shoulders, as if saying it's up to me now what I do. And I've always been a man of my word — no sense in changing that reputation now. And the way she's lookin' at me has me ready to burst in my damn jeans. She's gotta stop giving me all that fire. Makes a man weak.

I bridge the gap between us and grab onto her hips, giving her a swift tug to the end of the bench. She squeals and tries to fight me, but I'm too fast and far stronger. She trips out onto her feet, and I take the opportunity to bend down and grab hold of her arm.

When I stand back up, she's bent at the waist and thrown over my shoulder. Her little fists beat on my ass, but I ignore it.

"Was nice seein' you, Sawyer." I nod at him.

"See ya Monday," he says, tipping his drink in my direction. "You owe me for this, by the way."

"I figured."

"I hate both of you," River grumbles.

Everyone in the restaurant is lookin' at us until I turn and meet their gazes. I just smile and give a wave as I carry her out of Rudy's, sporting a hard-on that I can't even be bothered to be ashamed about. Giving her ass a little pat once we're outside, I carry her down Main Street until we come to my truck. Not a lot of people give us a second glance. I guess when you grow up in a small town, everyone kind of knows how crazy you can be. This is just another weekend for them.

The door creaks when I open the door, and I give her a little toss onto the seat. She is immediately in fighting mode, trying to slide out and past me.

"You're gonna have to be faster than that, darlin'." I grab onto her waist and trap her between me and the truck.

"God!" She groans and shoves my chest. "I hate you."

"No, you don't." I grin down at her and lean in closer.

"I do." Her wall is crumbling. "I really do, Hayes."

She's stopped fighting me for now, so I let my hands roam up her body, the dips and curves of her soft figure. Fuck, it feels good to touch her. I wonder if she's as wet for me as I am hard for her. My fingers tangle in her hair, and I tug her head back to force her to look up at me.

"Let me kiss you, firefly." My thumb runs across her lips, which part on a sigh.

"Hayes." She searches my gaze, her eyes worried and hopeful at the same time. "Please don't break my heart."

"Never again," I promise.

And then I kiss her.

CHAPTER NINETEEN

River

HOLY SHIT. He did it. He did pretty much exactly what Evie had suggested the other night, and my head is spinning. I should be furious with him for coming in like that to ruin my date and carry me out like I'm his property.

But if I'm being honest, it *really* turned me on. The way he ate me up with those gorgeous stormy eyes and threw me over his shoulder like a caveman. Shit, I was a goner. I didn't even think twice about Sawyer once I was dragged out of that restaurant.

Halfway back to his house, I called out of work. It's the first time I have ever called out, so they were pretty understanding, even though I know it's going to be busy. But there was no other choice. There's nowhere I would rather be than here with Hayes, trying to figure out where this is going.

"This is yours?" I gasp as I walk through the front of his house. I've never seen it, having passed up on the offer the last time I was here.

"Yep."

I glance back at him, and he's looking almost shy as he leans his back against the front door. The house is gorgeous on the inside. It reminds me so much of his parents' home, just updated and a bit brighter. It's got a farmhouse layout, with wide hallways and a huge living room that leads into the kitchen. It's decorated with cozy colors and so many pictures of his family.

Running my hand along the fireplace mantle, I see something that stops me in my tracks. There's a picture with a white wood frame, and it's of us. We were probably in our senior year, and he's kissing my cheek while I smile at the camera. And then a little farther down, there's a picture of me and Addie cuddled up on the couch while we read. I touch it lightly, my heart cracking wide open for this man.

My walls have officially crumbled.

"Couldn't let you go," he says behind me, his voice low and rough. "You or Addie."

His hands wrap around my waist, and I lean back into his embrace. He nudges my head to the side, and his mouth drops down to my neck, where he pushes my hair gently out of the way. Goose bumps break out across my skin, and my clit is throbbing with need. The way he touches me makes my thighs clench.

"I know everything about you, River Larson," he whispers, his breath ghosting across my jaw. "But I don't know anything when it comes to your body, and —*fuck*—I am ready to learn. Will you teach me?"

His rough palm runs across my collarbone and over my breasts, his fingers taking the time to roll and pinch at my nipples. My hips roll back to grind my ass against his cock, which is hard and pushing against his jeans. And then his hand dips lower, until he passes my zipper and cups me through my jeans. I moan and seek more pressure while his mouth nips and licks at my throat.

"Tell me what you want, River." He spins me around and grabs my jaw with one hand while his other moves to my ass. "Let me make this perfect for you."

My panties are soaked, and the tight seam of my jeans is doing little to relieve the throbbing there. I wrap my arms around his neck and pull him down into a kiss, our mouths opening and tongues sliding against one another's.

We've kissed before, in the middle of that muddy field and outside the restaurant. Those were hurried and frantic, where this is slow and soul shattering. My entire body responds to the slightest touch by him, every nerve lighting up with each swipe of his tongue or flex of his fingers. My blood is on fire.

"Take me to your room," I beg him. "Please."

He doesn't wait, bending over to pick me up so I'm straddling his hips. I hook my ankles behind him and run my hands through his soft hair. It's so much longer than I'm used to, but I love having something to hold on to.

His steps are sure as we walk back through the living room and up the stairs to his bedroom. The curtains are open, letting the setting sun come in through the windows. His bed is huge and filled with so many pillows and thick blankets that I know I would get the best sleep of my life in here.

"Alright, firefly." Hayes lets me slide down his body until I'm standing in front of him. He leans back onto the dresser and nods toward the bed in front of him and behind me. "Strip for me."

The butterflies in my stomach are going wild. I've never been this nervous to strip in front of a man before. I thought maybe it would be easier, seeing as I've known him for my entire life, but no. If anything, I think it's made it more difficult. But this is Hayes. So I take a deep breath and do as he says, fighting past the anxiety.

First, I kick off my heels and gently nudge them to the side. Then I grab the hem of my top and slowly pull it off, giving him ample time to watch as my breasts get lifted with my arms, almost spilling out of my lace bralette. My long hair falls back over my shoulders, and I toss the shirt off to the side.

I'm incredibly thankful that, for some reason, I decided to wear sexy underwear. It's not that I thought Sawyer would be getting lucky. I'm not the type of girl that sleeps with someone on the first date. But there's just something about wearing sexy underthings…it gives you serious confidence.

Hayes' eyes are glued to my body, and as I unbutton my jeans and tug down the zipper, his gaze moves south, watching me as I slip out of my jeans. I take a step back toward the bed and kick my jeans toward Hayes, who doesn't even notice. He's too busy looking at me like he's ready to eat me up.

He licks his lips, and I feel the bed touch my knees behind me, so I sit down and lean back on my hands, giving him a nice view of my entire body. My bra and panties match, both lace and a deep green color. I like the way the thong sits high on my hips, giving me the illusion of a smaller waist.

"Fuck," he says on an exhale. "You are stunning."

Kicking off his boots, he begins to strip as well. I've seen him practically naked a lot in my life. Hell, I even got a glimpse of his tight ass once when he was running out of the stream back in high school. We were skinny-dipping, and I had promised to close my eyes… But that was when he was a boy. Life has given him over ten years to work hard and hone those muscles.

He tugs off his Henley and unbuttons his jeans. I love the smattering of hair over his chest and the trail on his stomach that leads down to his cock. He's hard, and I can see how big he is from here. Dear god, I'm worried he won't fit.

"Eyes are up here, darlin'," he teases.

"But the show is down there." I look up at him and bite my lip.

Instead of continuing to undress, he just grins and drops to his knees. I raise a brow but remain silent, wondering what it is he's doing. And then he begins to crawl. On his goddamn hands and knees, he crawls over to me, his eyes never leaving mine.

I've never had a man *crawl* for me. I'm normally the one doing the crawling, or at least being the more submissive one. But the rush this gives me is unlike anything else. I like seeing him on his knees for me. It calls to my inner brat.

"River," he murmurs, running his stubble up my calf and kissing my knee. "Please tell me you forgive me."

He nudges my thighs apart and continues kissing up the sensitive flesh there. I am soaked, and my clit is pulsing, just begging for his attention. But he moves agonizingly slow, just barely touching me with his lips and tongue.

"Please, River." He bites me gently. "I'm so sorry. I promise I will never break us again. Please forgive me."

One of my hands goes to his hair, fisting it gently to urge him on.

"I forgive you," I tell him, watching as he grins up at me. "I forgive you. Just, please, touch me."

He hums and uses his hands to spread me wide, and I fall back onto my elbows. I watch him as he just stares at me, his strong hands massaging my thighs, getting closer and closer until I feel like I'm going to scream with need.

"You smell fucking divine. Do you know that, firefly?" His face dips down, and he runs his nose over my lace-covered slit. "Fucking heavenly. And it's all for me."

CHAPTER TWENTY

Hayes

I PUSH her sexy little panties to the side, and she is dripping for me. Using the tip of my finger, I run through her wetness and circle her clit. She moans and drops back flat on the bed, throwing her arms over her face.

"None of that," I tell her, pulling my finger away until she looks back down at me. "I want you to watch as I devour this sweet little pussy of yours, River. Watch me while I make you come."

"God, you've got a mouth on you. You know that?"

As an answer, I lick right up her seam and suck hard on her clit. Her hips jerk off the bed, and she lets out a sharp cry from the pleasure. Wrapping my arms around her hips, I hold her greedy pussy to my mouth, devouring her like she's my final meal.

"I think you like my mouth, firefly."

She moans again when I dip my tongue inside of her, tasting her arousal. Fuck, she tastes good. I could drown in her, eating her out until she has so many orgasms she can't walk. I don't even need to get off. This is enough.

One of her hands shoots back to my hair, tugging it hard enough to make my eyes water. But it just urges me on, and I lock eyes with her while snaking a hand back between her thighs to slip a single finger inside of her. Those sexy lips part as she rotates her hips, searching for more.

"Do you like this, River?" I ask, teasing her with soft strokes of my tongue as my finger slips in and out of her.

She nods and bites her bottom lip, her eyebrows pulled together as she watches me.

"What about this?" I add another finger, and then another, stretching her as I suck her clit into my mouth and tease it with the tip of my tongue.

"Oh, god," she groans. "Fuck, Hayes. I'm gonna come."

I don't answer, just keep doing what I'm doing. My fingers move sloppily inside of her, making obscene noises echo through the bedroom. Her stomach is heaving with each gasping breath, and before long, her pussy strangles my fingers, pulsing hard around them as her orgasm racks through her.

I watch it all, from the way her eyes roll back to the

way her other hand curls into the sheets. Her body is damp with sweat, and I can see her nipples poking out against the lace, begging to be sucked and bitten.

"Hayes." She takes a deep breath as I pull back from her thighs and begin to strip off the rest of my clothes. "That was…phenomenal. My god."

River props herself up on her elbows, giving me a gorgeous view of her flushed face and wild hair. She watches me as I shove my jeans down my legs and then do the same with my boxer briefs. My cock stands out, hard and so fucking ready, from my body. And I love the way she stares as I stroke myself.

"I think it's my turn," she says, her voice raspy with lust.

She licks her lips and slides down the bed, onto her knees. Fuck, the sheer sight of her on her knees for me is enough to do me in. It'll be a miracle if I don't blow within the first five seconds.

And then her hands are wrapping around my base while she leans in to lick the sticky precum from my tip. My toes fucking curl. It should be illegal to feel this good. She hums when I collect all of her inky hair into my fist and begin to guide her up and down my shaft.

Those full lips of hers struggle to take me, and when I hit the back of her throat, it takes her a second to let me slip past. I make some incoherent noises as I lift up onto my tiptoes, all of the muscles in my body tightening and singing with pleasure. I pull her off with a *pop*, and she wipes the corners of her mouth while she stares up at me, a knowing little grin on her face.

"What's wrong, Hayes?" she asks, her nails running up and down my thighs. "Been a while?"

"Oh, River," I say, laughing as I pull her up off her knees. "You are so gonna pay for that."

"Oh no." She pouts, sticking out the full bottom lip before turning around to face the bed. As she crawls on top of it, giving me an amazing view of her plump ass, she looks back at me. "Are you going to spank me, Hayes?"

She wiggles her hips, and I almost come at the sight. Fuck, where has this River been my whole life?

I crawl onto the bed next to her and pick her up, laying her over my lap. My cock is standing stiff between my stomach and her waist as she hangs over my thighs. She's propped herself up on her forearms, looking back at me with lust in her deep blue eyes. The amount of trust I see there fills my stomach with warmth.

"You like to be spanked, River, baby?" I ask her as I rub my palm over the curve of her ass.

She nods.

"Use your words, please."

"Yes." Pink splotches appear on her cheeks, and she struggles to meet my gaze.

"You like it a little rough, firefly?"

"God, Hayes." She takes a deep breath. "Don't make me say it."

"Because I do," I tell her, slipping a finger between her thighs. My cock twitches when I feel just how soaked she is.

"Yes." She moans as I circle her swollen clit. "Yes, I like it rough."

"Good." I pull my hand back and land a smack on her ass, causing her to jump. "Good girl, River."

I smack her again, this time on the other side, her cheeks pinkening up nicely.

"Fuck," she groans.

"But you tell me if you don't like anything or if we need to stop." I smack her again. "And we stop immediately. Okay?"

Another smack.

"Okay."

She collapses on the bed, her face buried in the covers, while one of my hands tangles in her hair and the other continues her punishment. I've never been this hard in my life, watching her pretty skin darken with each handprint while she moans and drips for me. She's fucking beautiful, and the sweet moans and whimpers she's making as we continue are just music to my fucking ears.

Once her ass is fully red and I don't want to push her any further, I soothe the heated skin with my palm.

She shifts and fidgets on my lap, pressing her thighs together as I move lower and lower.

"I love how desperate you are for me, baby."

I finally give her what she wants, plunging two fingers deep inside of her. Her back arches, and she cries out in pleasure. I fuck her slowly, teasing her closer and closer to the orgasm she's so desperate for.

"Please," she begs. "Please make me come, Hayes."

"You want to come all over my fingers?" I ask her. "Or would you prefer my cock?"

My thumb slips between her cheeks and applies the slightest pressure to her ass, and the responding hiss of breath lets me know she's interested. Good. Because I intend to own every part of her.

"Both," she says with a grin, glancing back at me.

"Greedy, greedy."

I wrap her hair in my fist and pick up the pace of my fingers, fucking her hard while my thumb continues to apply pressure to her backside. She's writhing and moaning on top of me, our bodies so close together that her movements stroke my cock. My precum drips down my shaft, lubricating it until my hips try to thrust against her.

"Yes," she hisses. "Right there."

"Come for me, darlin'."

Within seconds, she's there, her pussy clamping around my fingers as her breathing stutters and her muscles seize. When she falls limp, I lift her up and lay her on her back. She's sweaty and spent and so fucking beautiful. I make quick work of her panties, tugging them down her legs so she's bare for me.

River stares up at me with heavy-lidded eyes and a warm smile. Christ, she looks at me like I hung the moon for her. And when she reaches out for me, her thighs parting so I can crawl between them, my heart skips a beat.

"Come here," she murmurs.

CHAPTER TWENTY-ONE

Hayes

"YOU'RE BEAUTIFUL. Do you know that, firefly?" I let my body rest on top of hers, my forearms on either side of her sweet face. "Every inch of you is perfect."

Her hands run up my sides and then around to my back before I feel her nails gently scratch down my back. It makes my hips flex forward, the head of my cock pressing at her slick entrance.

"So are you," she says, adjusting her hips to a better angle. "I've always thought so."

"I'm sorry it took me so long to catch up." I kiss her, our lips moving together slowly and gently. I lick at the seam of her lips, and she opens for me to let our tongues dance together.

"Make up for it now," she says with a smirk as her hips lift to just the right angle. My head slips inside of her, and I groan, thinking of anything but the beautiful woman below me to keep my orgasm under control.

Slowly, agonizingly so, I sink inside of her. Her pussy stretches around me, and it's a tight fucking fit. Once I'm in to the hilt, I swear I see fucking stars as she clenches around me. Her breathing is labored as she works to relax and adjust. I kiss her cheeks, her forehead, and her throat as I murmur how fucking good she feels and how beautiful and sweet she is.

After a minute, she's relaxed and begins to rotate her hips a bit, testing how I fit inside of her. It's tight, and wet, and so fucking good.

"Do you know how good you feel, darlin'?" I pull out and slowly thrust back in, relishing the way I fit so perfectly inside of her.

"You're so big." She groans as I thrust again. "You're going to split me in half."

I chuckle and grab one of her legs to open her up farther, letting me go even deeper. Her back arches, and her head rolls back.

"Oh, god."

"I like that." I kiss up the side of her throat, feeling her pulse thrum beneath my lips. "You crying out to god while I'm inside of you."

"Cocky bastard." She laughs.

Her heel digs into my ass, getting leverage to lift her hips higher as I pick up my pace, thrusting into her hard and deep. I refuse to come before I get one more from her. And from the way her nails are digging into my back and her breathing is picking up…she's close.

I tug down the flimsy lace of her bra and take one of her nipples into my mouth. I tease and suck and bite and then do the same with the other. She's writhing beneath me, her hips meeting me each time I drive deep. I'm losing my focus. She feels so good — too good.

"I — I'm — Hayes!" she shouts as she comes, her nails biting deep into my skin.

The pain just makes the pleasure skyrocket, and the heat that had been building deep in my spine explodes through my body. My balls tighten, and her cunt squeezes me for all I'm worth as I empty myself into her. She tugs my face to hers, and we kiss as we both come back down to Earth.

"I've died and gone to heaven," I tell her, collapsing on top of her sweaty body. "Your pussy is the golden gate to my own personal heaven."

"Hayes!" She laughs and pushes me off her. Sort of. I'm too heavy for her to actually move, but I roll over nonetheless. "That's so wrong."

"What?" I kiss her shoulder and smile over at her. "It is."

"You're so wrong for that." But she's still laughing, and I'm blissed the fuck out.

"There is nothing wrong about this," I tell her, my hand going back between her thighs, where my cum is currently leaking out of her. Hell if that doesn't get me hard all over again. And then it hits me. I came inside of her. We didn't even discuss birth control or anything. We got caught up in the moment, and holy shit, was I irresponsible.

"Shit, River." I pull my hand from between her thighs and look over at her smiling face. "I came inside of you."

"How irresponsible of you," she teases. When she sees my wide, worried eyes, she smiles and rolls her eyes. "I have an IUD. It's fine. I wouldn't have let you otherwise."

"What-if I'm riddled with diseases?" I'm acting shocked, but I know I'm clean, and I have full faith that she is as well. She's not irresponsible like that, but I am kind of surprised she didn't *ask*.

"I chose to trust you when you said you'd been in a dry spell. Also, I trusted you, *my best friend*, not to fuck me with a dirty dick."

I snort. "My dick is not dirty. How dare you, madame."

"Yeah, but your mouth is." She rolls over, resting half of her body on mine, and props herself up on her elbow. Her thumb brushes across my bottom lip. "Filthy things came out of these lips. Where'd that come from?"

"You bring it out of me," I tell her, smiling against her lips when she leans down to kiss me.

"You carried me out of a date." She rolls onto her back and laughs. "You literally threw me over your fucking shoulder and carried me out of that restaurant. We were in *public*!"

"I feel like I cannot be held responsible for any questionable acts when it comes to you." She laughs even harder. "You make me a bit crazy."

"You've been making me crazy since we were kids." Her voice is softer now, and she looks over at me. "Time for a taste of your own medicine."

"Well, you're mine now." I grab her and tug her back to my side. She curls into me, fitting perfectly in my arms and against my body. I kiss the top of her head and breathe in her scent. "That's all that matters."

"And all of Cane Creek knows, I'm sure."

"Word does tend to spread pretty quickly around here."

We sit in silence for a bit, the sun going down and the tree frogs coming out. The windows are open, letting a cool breeze waft into the room around us. It smells like cut grass and wet earth from the stream that runs behind my house. Part of the same stream River and I used to swim in as kids and teenagers.

"Remember when we used to go skinny-dippin'?" I ask her.

"Of course I do." She laughs softly. "Used to tell you I wouldn't look…"

"River Larson!" I gasp in mock outrage. "Did you betray my trust?"

"Only a little." She makes a little gesture with her fingers. "I just peeked. At your butt."

"Unforgivable."

"As if you never took a little look when I was swimming or walking back to the beach." She rolls her eyes. "Please."

"Never." Lies. "Not once."

I could see her body when she'd swim too close, her breasts bobbing under the water when she'd laugh. Back then, I was just a horny teenager, excited that I had a girl around me that was naked. I was too stupid to realize that maybe the happiness I always felt around her, that levity you get when you're truly comfortable with someone, was maybe there because I had love for her that extended past friendship.

Pops said sometimes mistakes have to be made to learn certain lessons, but this was a hard one to live with. It took too long, stole too much time. That mistake robbed us of over ten years together. And as I hold her now, I'm desperate to keep her close, to not fuck up all over again and lose her.

"You're a bad liar, Hayes Black." Her laughter fills the rooms. "But I like you anyway."

I kiss her temple. "I think we should do it again."

"Already? Don't you need a little more..." She gestures to my dick. "Time?"

"Not that." I roll my eyes and laugh, sitting up on

the bed. "Skinny-dipping. Although, I'm not opposed to round two if you'd prefer."

I wag my eyebrows at her, and she gives me a playful shove before rolling off her side of the bed.

"Last one there owes the other an orgasm!" She takes off out of the bedroom, and I give her a head start. Because honestly? There is nothing I'd like more than to owe that woman an orgasm…or five.

CHAPTER TWENTY-TWO

River

I REALIZE once I'm downstairs that he is deliberately not chasing me. Cheeky fucker is fine owing me an orgasm, but whatever. Not anything I'm going to get upset about. The ground is still warm from the sun, but the air is cool, and it feels amazing on my sweaty skin.

Taking a second to soak up the beautiful evening, I lean my head back and breathe deep. Living out in the middle of nowhere has its perks, including being able to walk out your front door naked and not worry about anyone catching a glimpse. At least, I hope none of his family decides to make a little visit.

Hayes has built a gorgeous home, with a big front porch and hanging plants that have grown to skim the railing. He's even got a daybed-type bench with a thick cushion and pillows. I could see myself sitting there, sipping on Katherine's sweet tea while Hayes walked home from working on the ranch, a smile on his face when he sees me.

I wonder what it would be like to be here with him, happy and loved.

"I gave you a very large head start." He's standing naked in the doorway, leaning against the frame with his arms crossed around a couple of towels. That huge cock of his is getting hard again, hanging heavy between his thighs. His entire body is hard, muscles formed from years of working on the ranch every day.

Fuck, he's a beautiful sight.

"Got distracted." I shrug.

"Stream's that way." He nods to his left, my right. But I already knew. I know this ranch like the back of my hand, and it doesn't escape me that he chose to build on land so close to the same stream we used to spend so much time in. Pretty sure, if I'm not all turned around, that this is the area where we used to escape to practice our dancing.

I take off running again, and I can hear him this time, trying to catch up with me. His breathing is heavy, and twigs break under our feet as we race to the water. I can hear it running, and my heartbeat pounds in my ears. I glance over my shoulder, and he's close, so close that he could easily reach out and grab me. I squeal and laugh, picking up my pace to get out of his grasp.

Finally, the water comes into view, and I run into it without thinking. And holy shit, it is cold. I forgot how frigid the water coming from the mountains can be, and it steals my breath as I trip and stumble until I fall in with a splash. And then Hayes is there, grabbing my body out of the water, laughing in my face about how I just fell face-first into the stream.

"You really wanted that orgasm, didn't you, darlin'?"

I give him a shove and wrap my legs around his to push him under. But he's too tall and catches himself as he falls backward, saving his head from going under. He laughs, and I straddle his waist, desperate to dunk him below the surface. But goddamn, this man is strong and relentless.

"It's only fair!" I shout between my laughter. "Dunk yourself, you butthole!"

"That is uncalled for!" He can barely breathe he's laughing so hard, and I use it to my advantage, tripping him up until his head *finally* goes under the water.

"Okay, okay!" He spurts, coming up for air. "We're even."

He grins at me, his smile making the sides of his eyes crinkle and the ghost of one dimple appear. My heart stutters at how handsome he is. I spent the last decade thinking I would never be here again, that I would never get to be close to him like I used to be. And now this? I am freaking giddy with it.

"You're too handsome for your own good. You

know that?" I ask him as he leans back to wet his hair, slicking it out of his face.

"I always thought I was just the right amount."

I shove him playfully and squirm out of his grip. I dip down under the water again, smoothing my hair back and appreciating the cool water on my face. God, I miss this. You don't get this kind of living in the city.

"You remember dancin' just over there?" he asks, gesturing off in the distance through the trees.

I hum.

"I thought we were close to where we used to practice." I swim back over to him. "That on purpose, Mr. Black?"

I'm teasing him, even though there's a part of me that really hopes that's true, that maybe he was thinking about me all these years just like I was thinking about him. It seems silly to hope that maybe he was carrying a torch for me or something.

But then he tugs me close and looks at me as he shrugs. His eyes have gone all soft and sweet, making my stomach flip-flop.

"Pops asked where I wanted to build…what piece of land I wanted. And we have so much of it, and you know, I left for a while and never really fit in here like Rhett and Wells do. Hell, even Dean fits in better than I do when he's sober and home. So I think he thought I'd want to be as far away as possible."

"You could've gone off in the woods." I play with

the ends of his hair at the base of his neck. "I remember you talking about becoming a forest recluse, hidden away in the foothills of the mountains. Only coming out for work."

"And Momma's cookin'," he adds. "I thought about it. But I like this little piece of land. I can walk to Rhett's and Momma's. And you're here."

"I'm here *now*," I say, rolling my eyes. "Wasn't here when you built it."

"You were always here, River," he says. "In the stream, on the land. You were sittin' on the front porch when I came home from work and making your cobbler on Sunday afternoons in the kitchen. You were out back next to the fire pit, making s'mores with the kids. You were everywhere, River. Always have been. Only place I couldn't find you was in my bed."

His smile turns ornery as hell.

"Stop that." I grab his face and really look at him, my eyes searching his. "Don't cheapen all that sweet stuff like that. Do you mean that? Or are those just pretty words to get you back in my good graces?"

"Is it so hard to believe that I wanted you back in my life?" His arms wrap even tighter around me, keeping me flush against him. "From the second you walked away, I knew I made the biggest mistake of my life. I wanted you back as soon as you walked out of my sight."

CHAPTER TWENTY-THREE

River

"THEN WHY NOT COME GET ME?" I'm trying hard not to let my emotions get the best of me, but as I look into his sincere blue eyes, I struggle to keep them under control. Things could have been so different if he had just come after me.

"I don't want to make excuses for myself, River. But I was young and stupid. I was angry and shocked that you just walked away. And not only that, but you avoided me all summer and then ran to the city. By the time I got my head out of my ass, you were gone."

"You should've moved faster," I grumble, laying my head on his shoulder. His laughter vibrates through me as I snuggle closer, and he spins us slowly in the water.

"I came to find you, ya know." He's speaking so low I think I mishear him at first.

"To the city?"

"Mhm," he hums. "I didn't tell anyone. Just took off a few months after you did. Asked your sister where you were living, and she very reluctantly gave up your address."

"Janie?" I pull back for a second and look at him. "She spoke to you? She never told me."

"Swore her to secrecy," he says, winking at me before gently cradling my head back to his shoulder. "Anyway, I drove all those hours to see you, rehearsing what I was gonna say the entire time."

"Oh, do tell."

"It's been a while. I can't really remember it all, but there was a lot of begging involved. *A lot* of begging. Groveling, actually. Being on my knees while I asked you over and over again to forgive me and come home."

We both laugh, and I try to imagine what it would've been like to have him chase after me. Would I have forgiven him? Gone back home with him? I think I would have. No matter how angry I still was back then, I think I would've followed him home without a second thought.

Back then, I was too young to realize that a man doesn't have to be your entire world just because you love him. It's possible to love someone and still have your own life with your own experiences, and I think I would've missed out on a lot had he gone through with it. Maybe we had to become different people to fit our pieces together.

"What happened?" I ask, curious as to what stopped him.

"I parked outside your apartment, and I sat there for a while. A very long while." He chuckles. "I think I was there for hours, just waiting and trying to decide what I was going to do. And then, you walked out. Your hair was pulled up in this wild, messy knot on top of your head, and you were in sweats, and...I don't know. You looked *sad*, River."

Not surprising. I was in a city where I didn't know anyone, and I had just had my heart broken by the man I loved for over half my life. Those first few months, or year rather, were an uphill climb. I had to start fresh, make all new friends, and be okay with living by myself and being alone. It was a lot for an eighteen-year-old to manage.

"And I thought, there's no way I can fix that." He kisses the top of my head. "I watched you, walking down the road to the corner shop, your head low and your face pale and sad. I just knew there was no good that could come of me trying to bring you back. I was still young, still a bit of an ass, and I knew I wasn't good enough for you."

"Yet," I add, laughing when he tries to smack my ass through the water.

"So I drove home." He shrugs. "Came back. No one knew except Janie, and I just pretended like it never happened. I left you to live your big life. I hoped you would move on, have all the big experiences you always wanted."

He clears his throat.

"I thought maybe you'd find someone who could treat you right and be the person you needed. I couldn't be that person, so I hoped someone else could be. Only ever wanted you to be happy, firefly. No matter how much it killed me to think it wouldn't be me."

"You're a good man, Hayes Black." I kiss his neck. "Now, anyway," I tease.

"I'll admit, I didn't change overnight."

"No shit?" My voice is just dripping with sarcasm.

"No shit," he agrees. "Took me a few years to get my shit under control. Dean kind of helped with that. I watched him throwing his life away, and I watched Rhett step up. And I thought, okay, I can do this. I'll try to go make something of myself and my music, do something that's just for me."

"And you hated it." I look up at him.

"Hated it." He laughs. "God, I hated the city. Only good thing about living there was the 2:00 a.m. pizza delivery."

"I do miss the late-night deliveries," I commiserate. "There was this amazing Thai place down the block that would deliver twenty-four seven. So fucking good."

"And yet all the food in the world couldn't keep me away when the ranch and Dean and everything just started going up in flames. I came home, worked hard, and decided to get my shit together."

"I'm very happy you did. I kinda like the man you are today."

"I bet you do." He smirks at me. "He is very good at giving you a lot of orgasms."

"Speaking of…" I pull away and start walking backward out of the water. His eyes dip to my breasts and then lower as my stomach and hips come out of the water. "I think you owe me one."

"That's right," he says, nodding slowly as he begins to follow me. My eyes dip down to his abs as he stalks me out of the water. "How would you like me to deliver said orgasm, River?"

My eyebrows knit together in a silent question.

"I'm only asking how you want it." He slowly follows me as I continue to walk backward. I glance over my shoulder and see the towels laying a few feet away, so I grab one before turning back to him.

"Do you want to come on my fingers?" he asks, stepping completely out of the water. His eyes are hungry, watching me wrap myself in a towel. It's freezing with the little breeze and cold water on my skin, and yet my blood is on fire as I watch him.

"Or my tongue, maybe? Let me taste you?"

Jesus Christ.

He walks up to me, standing only inches away. His hands go to where I'm clutching the towel around my body, and he gently tugs it away. I let it fall to the ground again and stand there as he looks me over. His knuckles run along my collarbone and then over my nipples before grazing lower and lower.

"Or maybe you want to feel that sweet stretch my cock gives you?" His eyes dart back up to mine for a second, and I lose my breath. "You want to come all over my cock again, firefly?"

One of his arms wraps around my middle, and the other sinks between my thighs. I'm already wet and needy for him as his fingers tease and explore. We're face-to-face, our eyes locked on each other's as his fingers stroke all the sweetest spots. My legs are weak, and there's an amazing heat building deep in my core.

And then he kisses me, and my world tilts on its axis. I will never get sick of this feeling.

"So?" he asks, pulling back while his fingers still move inside of me. "What'll it be?"

CHAPTER TWENTY-FOUR

River

I WAKE up the next morning, my body scraped and sore from our second round that happened right there next to the creek. I begged him to take me right there, to lay me on the ground and fuck me in the dirt and leaves.

And he did just that, rutting into me like a man on a mission to make my orgasm a good one. The pain from the little rocks and sticks bit into my back and ass, making the pleasure that much more intense. He kissed and licked and bit me all over my body as our hips rocked together frantically.

Our breath mingled, and he stared into my eyes as I came and as he followed soon after. We lay there for a minute, just soaking each other up and kissing over and over again. I mean, god damn, that man can kiss. And then he wrapped me up and carried me back inside, this time in his arms instead of over his shoulder.

"Riv?"

I roll over and stretch, but the bed is empty.

"Good morning."

Sitting up, I see him standing in the doorway, his Wranglers stretched tight over his thighs and a dirty white T-shirt clinging to his chest.

"It should really be illegal to look that good this early." I groan and fall back into the pillow.

"I brought you coffee," he says with a smile. "I'll set it here on your side for when you're ready."

My side.

"Stay in bed, darlin'. You have work today?" He sits down next to me, pushing my hair out of my face and looking at me in that way that makes my heart beat a little faster.

"Nope." I smile up at him. "I'm off all day. Shouldn't you be?"

"No rest for the wicked." He winks. "Rhett asked us yesterday if we'd help him over at his house. He's building a big-ass deck."

"Yeah?" I sit up and take the coffee in my hands. It's got plenty of milk, and when I take a sip, I realize he's added some hazelnut flavoring. My favorite.

"Hazelnut." He grins. "Bought it when you started lookin' in my direction again."

"Thought I'd be sleeping over, cowboy?"

He shrugs. "Anyway, the kids would love to see you, I'm sure. And Poppy. We'll all be over there if you want to come. Take your time, shower and change, and come over to join us."

"Change? Into what, may I ask?"

"Your clothes from yesterday are in the dryer. Washed them this morning while your lazy ass slept like a baby."

"I was recovering from the multiple orgasms you gave me last night." I smile at him and lean forward, asking for a kiss. He gives it to me, and he tastes like toothpaste and smells like his shampoo.

"Take your time. Sleep in if you want. It's still really early."

"Gathered that from the sun barely being up."

He leans in and kisses me again.

"You have no idea how long I've waited to see you here."

"In your bed?" I raise an eyebrow.

"In my house," he corrects. "In my bed is just a bonus. But I've always wanted to see you here. This place was empty without you."

"You sound pretty confident that this is what you want." I reach out and take his hand. "You said a lot last night about us, about me being in this house and in your life. We went from friends to whatever the hell we were for all those years, to now...this. Is this what you want?"

"Why would you think it isn't?"

"Because we moved at lightning speed." I give him

a reassuring smile. "If you're having second thoughts…"

He throws his head back, laughing with his whole chest.

"Shut up." He stands, giving me a kiss. "Meet me at Rhett's when you're ready to get your cute ass out of bed."

I watch him leave, a little confused and a lot happy.

<u>HAYES</u>

I take one of the four-wheelers over to Rhett's place since I have tools and shit to haul over, and it really doesn't take but a few minutes to get there. But the entire way over, I'm just thinking about how I've left River in my bed. Took all my strength to not blow off workin' today just to crawl back in bed with her.

She sat up and looked at me, surprise in her eyes like she didn't quite expect to be in my room still. Her black hair was sticking up everywhere, and I couldn't stop looking at the way the shadows around the room played on her body.

And when she asked me if I was having second thoughts… I could've handled that better. But I couldn't help but laugh at the suggestion. Me. Have second thoughts. About River fucking Larson. Never in a million years.

I may be a man who makes some rash decisions in life, but she is not one of them. I've had twelve years to get my shit together, think about what I did, and realize that River isn't someone I can lose a second time. Not only can I not lose her friendship, but I can't lose her love.

So that means there's no way in hell I would second-guess the decision to be with her. From the second I decided to walk into that restaurant and she turned her angry eyes on me, I knew this was the right thing to do. May not have been the best way to go about things, but got me to where I wanted to be in the end.

But I do realize my laughter and playful nature in that moment probably wasn't the best move. I'll have to make sure I properly quell her anxieties later. I shouldn't have laughed or made a joke out of it, and I'll make that right when she comes over to Rhett's.

"So..." Wells trails off as he takes a break from hammering boards.

"So?" I ask, looking in his direction. "What can I help you with, little brother?"

"Didn't see you at dinner yesterday evenin'." Rhett's gruff voice cuts into Wells' procrastinating. Very much like Rhett to just cut to the chase. "Or River at the bar last night."

"Heard about a little public display of affection..." Wells is fighting back a grin.

"Yeah, I may have momentarily lost my goddamn mind yesterday."

That gets both Rhett and Wells laughing.

"Your woman will do that to ya," Rhett says, his rare smile lingering on his face. Didn't used to be rare. Back when we were growin' up, I feel like he was smiling and laughing more than any of us, always cracking jokes and goofing off. I guess Dean and Addie really put a damper on all that.

"I'm guessin' you took her straight back to your house, then? Seeing as you *also* weren't at the bar."

I look over to Wells and nod, a stupid grin flooding my face. "You've no idea how happy it makes me to say she's in my bed right now." My goofy grin keeps getting bigger.

"She see all those pictures of herself in your house?" Rhett asks.

"There's literally, like, two. You make it sound as if I have a shrine in my closet like Helga from *Hey Arnold!*"

I get an amused grunt in response.

"I don't think I've ever seen you this happy." Wells comes up next to me and gives me a hard squeeze on the shoulder. "Don't fuck it up."

"You work through your shit with her?" Wells and I both look over at Rhett. He's watching me closely, his eyes narrowed like he means business.

"We did," I tell him. Because we have. "For the most part anyway."

I don't know why I say it out loud. This has not been something that's played on my mind every minute of every day. It's not an issue. Not a really big one anyway. It's just something that's been lurking in the back of my mind since she came back to town, since we started looking each other's way again.

"For the most part?" Wells turns to me with a confused look.

"Look, it's not that big of a deal. I don't know why I even said anything. Forget it." I wipe the sweat from my brow and try to get back to work.

I should've known by calling it *not that big of a deal* that Rhett and Wells would immediately make it a big deal.

"If you're mentioning it, then it means something," Wells says.

"And by not talking about it, it just becomes a very large elephant in a very small room," Rhett adds. He sits down on one of the folding chairs next to the skeleton of a deck. "So spill, little brother."

"He's the littlest." I point at Wells.

"And you're *littler* than me. That makes you little. Stop deflecting."

I roll my eyes.

"The whole Addie thing just bugs me. That's all. No big deal." I shrug and kick grass around with the toe of my boot. "I treated River like trash, and I made her feel like she couldn't even come back for her friend's funeral. That's on me. Not getting her support through that…is on me."

When I finally look up at them, they're looking at each other, a silent conversation going on that I am annoyingly not privy to.

"What?" I ask them both. "Why're y'all lookin' at each other like that?"

"Not our zoo, not our zebra," Rhett says with a grunt.

"The phrase is not our *circus*, not our *monkey*," I correct. "But what in the hell isn't exactly your monkey?"

"Uncle Hayes!" Jo singsongs as she prances out of the house, careful not to trip on the makeshift walkway. "River is here."

She's got a shit-eatin' grin on her face, probably remembering our conversation about how her dad and Poppy think I *like* like her.

"That girl is nothin' if not ornery as hell," Rhett mutters under his breath, standing up from his chair and giving us a single clap. "Time to get back to work."

Jo jumps off the decking as Wade hangs back in the doorway to watch us. His sister is off, runnin' full speed toward River, who is walking around the side of the house and all the tall hydrangea bushes that scent the air.

They must've been watching for her inside with Poppy. Shit fire, she looks good enough to eat. Her hair is still damp, hanging past her shoulders. I forgot she wore heels last night, so she's walked over here barefoot.

If it were anyone else, I'd worry about them walkin' that far without any shoes. But she's always been like that, barefoot and running around this ranch. It tugs all those memories of us back to the forefront, the issue about Addie tucked away. She looks like she belongs as Jo goes flying into her arms, fast friends.

I couldn't ask for more than this.

CHAPTER TWENTY-FIVE

River

"RIVER!" Jolene runs full speed at me, jumping into my arms as I swing her around. Guess we're close enough for this now since I let her and Wade eat far too much cobbler at the birthday party. "Are you here to help my uncles or play with me and Mommy? That's what I call Poppy now. She's our mommy."

Oh, the way my heart swells for this baby girl.

"And me!" Wade shouts. "Quit lumpin' me in with them," he says, pointing his thumb over his shoulder at the Black brothers, who are all looking very handsome in the sunshine.

"I am most definitely here to play with you guys," I tell her, my eyes lingering on the way Hayes' arm muscles are straining. He winks at me, and I blush, turning back to Jolene. "I'm not doing any kind of manual work on my day off."

"I have lemonade!" Poppy calls out from the kitchen. Jolene slides out of my arms and runs off toward her uncles and daddy.

Rhett's house has a window to the kitchen that he's converted to slide open to an outside bar. Once the deck is finished, they'll have a great place to entertain people. I walk over to it, climbing on the bare bones of the decking they're putting up. Poppy smiles when she sees me.

"Hey, *Mommy*," I say, smiling at her through the screen.

"I know, right?" She slides it open and sets the pitcher on the counter along with a tray of glasses. "I cried the first time she said it. I handed her a glass of water, and she just looked up at me and said, 'Thanks, Mommy', like it was the most natural thing in the world."

"I would've cried, too." I lift the tray off the bar, and Poppy comes outside, grabbing the pitcher of lemonade. Following her over to a large wooden outdoor table, we set the drinks down and take a seat.

"Rhett made this," she says, running her hand along the smooth wood. "I asked him if we could make an area outside so we could have the family over. Two days later, this thing is sitting out here. And a few days later, he started on the deck."

"It's gorgeous. It's going to be perfect out here." I lean back and try desperately not to look over at Hayes.

But I can feel his stare like a damn brand. He's watching me. "So…do you live here now?"

She goes as pink as her hair as she shrugs.

"Kind of." She looks past me, presumably at Rhett and the kids. "Most of my stuff is here, and I spend most nights here. I was worried about moving too fast for the kids, but every night I try to go back to my little cabin, they get sad. And that kind of rips my heart into pieces."

"So, move in." I shrug.

"Probably will. We went and picked out rings the other day." Her eyes go all wet and dreamy. I'm thrilled for her. They just seem so fucking happy together. "We'll do a little trial run living together after the fair in a couple weeks. The kids will be back in school, and we'll see how they do with me being a permanent fixture in their life."

"I'm sure Rhett can't wait to have you in his bed every night."

"Speaking of beds," she says, clearing her throat and leaning forward, her elbows on the table. "I hear you may not have been in your own last night?"

Good god. Word travels faster than lightning.

"And how would you know that?"

"Hayes wasn't at family dinner." She shrugs. "And you weren't at the bar."

"I want to glance over my shoulder right now to make sure he isn't paying attention to us," I tell her.

"But I'm pretty sure he is, and I don't want his ego to grow even bigger when he sees us talking about him."

Her eyes slide past me and then back.

"How would he know we're talking about him?" she whispers.

"Who else would we be whispering about?"

"Keep talkin' about me, darlin'!" Hayes shouts, making me jump out of my skin. "Make sure you tell her all the good stuff."

I raise a hand in the air, not even bothering to turn around, and stick my middle finger up high. They all laugh behind me, and I roll my eyes.

"What's she doin'?" I hear Wade's little voice ask.

"Saluting your uncle," Wells says, laughing.

"It's not a nice salute," Rhett adds. "Even if it is warranted."

"You're the brightest shade of red I think I've ever seen." Poppy's smile is contagious.

"Fine," I groan, admitting defeat. "I *may* not have been in my own bed last night."

She squeals and gets out of her seat to come sit next to me. Grabbing a glass of lemonade, she scoots up close and lays her hand on my forearm.

"Tell. Me. Everything."

"Well, he showed up at my date."

"No, he didn't," she whispers, scooting even closer.

"He did. Interrupted us before we even finished our

food. Carried my ass out over his shoulder like he was staking some stupid alpha claim on me."

"Rhett did that to me once," she tells me, grinning like an idiot. "Woof. When I tell you I melted for the man the moment he threw me over his shoulder… Just knowing he could lift me up like that was a promise he'd be fun in the bedroom."

"Oh, my god." I laugh with her as she erupts into a fit of giggles.

"Seriously! That shit is hot."

"Maybe in the privacy of your own home. He did this *in public*, Poppy. In front of half the damn town."

"You're exaggerating." She playfully rolls her eyes. "Twenty-five percent. Maybe."

"Anyway," I continue. "Then he kissed me senseless, apologized profusely, and took me back to his house."

"How was it?" She wags her eyebrows at me.

I glance over my shoulder, and Hayes is playing with Jolene. So I lean back in toward Poppy.

"He kind of rocked my world."

She tries to contain her excitement, quietly squealing and squeezing my arm.

"He was incredibly attentive, extraordinarily kind, and very, very *blessed*, if you know what I mean." I can feel the blush spread across my cheeks. "I'm surprised I'm not walking with a limp."

Poppy bursts out laughing, throwing her hand over

her mouth.

"That's not the reaction she should be having!" Hayes shouts over at us. "Not a fan of the laughing! What're you tellin' her, River?"

"Mind your business!" I call back over my shoulder before turning my attention to Poppy. "You know he had pictures of me in his house?"

"Shut up."

I nod. "One of us together and then one of me and Addie. Right there above his fireplace, like I was a main feature in his life."

"Maybe you were, River." Her voice has gone all soft. "Maybe he's been waiting for you to come back."

I tell her about everything he told me — about coming to the city to find me, about why he built the house where he did, and all the sweet things he said to me last night. How he crawled on his knees, begging my forgiveness and promising never to hurt me again. She listens to everything, soaking it all up with wide eyes and excitement.

Saying it all out loud makes it far more real, and when I look back over my shoulder, I see him watching me instead of working. He grins, and my heart does a couple of little flips. Then he winks, and I have to turn back around because I can't stand him looking at me like that in public.

"He's looking at you like he's ready for the next round."

I snort and slap her for that comment.

"What?" She shrugs, taking a sip of her lemonade. "He does. So what happens now?"

"What do you mean?" I lean forward and pour my own glass.

"Everything okay now?" she asks. "You guys worked everything out, and you're not mad at him and he's not upset with you?"

"I'm not mad at him." I avoid the last part of her question.

"You told him, right?" Her voice drops low. "About you coming back, even though he doesn't remember it?"

"Uh, negative."

"You should tell him, River." Her eyes look worried. "Do you really want him to keep thinking you didn't come home for Addie?"

I sigh and feel anxiety coil in my stomach. She's right. I need to tell him. He deserves to know, even if he'll hate that I saw him like that. Even though he could end up hating me for abandoning him when he needed me most.

But we're in this happy little bubble right now, where everything we're experiencing is new and fun. I don't want to throw cold water on it and ruin what we have going for us. I can tell him later, when we're more comfortable, better established in whatever it is we are.

"I'll tell him."

"He's not going to leave you for that." Her gaze

softens. "I can see all that worry written all over your face."

"You don't know that," I whisper, the emotions causing my throat to seize. "You don't know. It could be another nuclear explosion."

"I think if you're going to make this work, you're going to have to learn to trust each other all over again." She gives me a tight smile. "This will never work if you're worrying he could leave you any day on a whim."

"Not on a whim," I correct her, chancing another look back at Hayes. "This wouldn't be on a whim."

"Either way." She sighs. "I love this. I love you two. And I want to see you succeed. I want to see how cute your babies are."

Her eyes turn playful again.

"I think babies are quite a ways off."

Poppy shrugs as Jolene runs up to the table, hopping up in Poppy's lap.

"Maybe. But I'm excited nonetheless."

Jolene grabs a glass of lemonade and chugs it down like it's her first drink in a month. Once it's gone, she gives a heavy sigh and leans back into Poppy.

"I'm havin' a good day." Her little head cranes back, and she looks up at Poppy. "How about you, Mommy?"

"Oh, sweet girl," Poppy says, her eyes going watery as she kisses Jolene on the forehead. "I'm having the best day ever now that you're in my arms."

CHAPTER TWENTY-SIX

Hayes

I'VE SPENT the entire week with River, hiding away in the rescue barn for the hours she's here. And then if she's working, I go to the bar and sit on a stool at the end of the line, watching to make sure no one gets too comfortable with her. I'm fine with her being sweet enough to make tips, but the second one of them decides to take it a step further, maybe touch her in some way, I will pounce.

So far, it's been okay. But I'm watching them.

And then at night, she hops in my truck or follows me back to the ranch in her Jeep, and we spend the night together. She hasn't been back at her mom's house since last weekend, and everything in my house smells like her now. My T-shirts she wears to bed, my sheets, my couch. Hell, I can smell her sweet honeysuckle scent even just walking into the house after she's been there.

I never want her to leave. I keep tryin' to get the nerve up to ask her to move in, but Wells and Rhett have both told me to slow the fuck down. I'm jumping into everything too quickly, they say. But they don't feel what I feel for River. They don't have our past. I *know* River, and I know I want to be with her.

Getting her out of that house with her mother is high on my list. When she moved back, she went straight to living with her mom so she could help pay the bills and get the creditors off her mom's back. But she needs her own space. She's a grown-ass woman and deserves to have a quiet place to come home to every night, where there isn't a mother ready to yell at her for god knows what.

River's dad died when she and her sister, Janie, were young. He was coming home late from a work thing, and a drunk driver hit him almost head-on as he was winding through the back roads. I remember River calling us that morning, telling Momma and Pops what happened and her asking them if they could come get her. Her mom was a wreck and didn't want to even look at her kids, let alone help them process the grief.

Janie had gone to a friend's house, and when Momma and I pulled up to get River, she ran out, hiccoughing back tears as she threw herself into Momma's arms. I've never seen someone so devastated, so just absolutely wrecked. I was young, but I could tell a part of River died that day with her dad. She was sad for so, so long. I even catch glimpses of it sometimes to this day.

And I don't know why her momma blames the kids for his death, but she does — always has.

That's why River always spent so much time over here with us. She needed parental figures who could give her love and who were willing to take her in when shit got too rough. There were many times in high school that River would come over, her face streaked red from crying, and ask to sleep over with Addie.

"How're things at your momma's?" I ask her. We're sitting in the rescue barn, playing and loving on Betty this afternoon.

She shrugs.

"About the same as always. Mom is drunk and angry. A ghost, really. I keep trying to tell her she's going to kill herself, but she doesn't care." River's eyes are sad when she looks up at me. "She just wants to be with Daddy."

"No excuse for treating you like she does."

"I know." She sighs and leans her head back on the wall. "But that doesn't mean I don't love her. She's my mom, and before Daddy died, I have a few great memories with her. I can't just turn that off, and I can't let her lose everything and wind up homeless or something."

I understand that. God, we all feel the same way about Dean. No matter how many times Dean fell off the wagon or came home angry and drunk, we picked him up and loved him through it. Even when Pops kicked him out, it was out of love, trying to knock some sense into his thick skull, set him right.

But how much guilt is River supposed to feel for the death of her father? How long can she be expected to endure that kind of hate from her momma?

"You're always welcome at mine, you know."

"I've been at your house every day this week, Hayes." She grins. "I figured if you had an issue with it, you would've kicked me out by now."

"I'm thinkin' you should bring some stuff over. Toothbrush, some clothes…everything you own…"

She closes her eyes and shakes her head at me.

"Are you subtly trying to ask me to move in with you, Hayes Black?"

"Gross. No." I scoff. "I don't want your girly shit all up in my space. No."

She laughs, and Betty gets excited, standing on River's thighs as she tries to lick her face. Which just makes River laugh harder, and I'm just sitting here watching them both, loving how far they've come since Betty had her accident.

"I think you're almost ready to take her home with you."

"I was hoping to have my own place by the time she was ready," River says once Betty has settled back down at our sides. "I've been looking, but Cane Creek does not have a lot of places for rent. And since you don't want my girly shit all up in your space…"

I wink at her.

"Move in with me."

"Hayes." She sounds cautious, maybe a little exasperated by me. "It's too early. And you know it's too early."

"Please." I roll my eyes. "I've known you since we were kids." *And I love you.*

"No." She smiles and leans forward to lay a hand over mine. "Not yet. Just, give me some time, okay? I want to make sure we do this right."

"We are doing this right." I scratch Betty's favorite spot, a little soft area right behind her left ear. "There's no way we can do it wrong when it's me and you, Riv. But I'll respect your wishes. For now."

"Poppy hasn't even moved in with Rhett yet, and they're practically married."

"Bad example," I tell her. "Poppy basically lives there. I think she's spent the night at her little cabin like once since they told the kids. Rhett says Jolene and Wade get too upset when she goes to leave, and she ends up stayin'."

"Yeah, well, they've had longer than us to decide it's what they want."

"We've had since we were six."

She snorts. "There is no winning with you."

"Nope." I smile big and lean forward to grab her hands. Giving her a firm pull, I move her on top of my thighs so she's straddling me. Betty doesn't even flinch. Just lies there and watches us as she tries not to drift off.

"I'm not saying I don't want this to go somewhere," she says softly, running her fingers through my five-o'clock shadow. "I do. I *really*, really do. And I want to say yes to moving in with you."

That really gets me smilin'. Maybe she's gonna give in.

"But…" she continues, and I deflate a little. "I want to go a bit slower than that. I just…"

"Tell me, firefly. You can tell me anything." I kiss her palm.

"I'm actively trying not to let what happened in our past dictate what or how I feel in the present. But it does. There's a lot of trust to rebuild there."

She pauses, looking a bit worried. Like she isn't sure she should keep going, but I can take it. I want to hear all of her anxieties and thoughts so I can help her work through them.

"I'm still a little worried that I'm just the flavor of the month." She cringes when she says it. "It's a very, very small part of my brain that's saying that. But it's there, and I can't seem to make it shut up."

"I think that's okay." I hold her tight. "I think after everything we've been through, I have a lot to make up for, and your brain is just reminding you of that. I don't like that you feel that way, but it just makes me more determined to prove that brain of yours wrong."

Her smile wavers, and for a second, I think she has more to say. But whatever it was, it's gone quickly, and she's leaning in to kiss me.

"I gotta go get ready for work," she mumbles against my lips. But I don't want to let her go. I hold her tighter, my fingers digging into her ass while her hands try to gently push me away.

"I'd prefer you just stay here. We can find something a bit more fun to do…"

"I am approaching the barn!" Wells' voice drifts in through the wide-open doors. "I repeat, I am approaching the barn!"

"You think I'm gonna let him do anything inappropriate in public like this?" she asks him as he walks inside. "Please. I have a little more class than that."

"I know you do," Wells tells her as she climbs up off my lap. "But he doesn't."

"I've got work tonight, so I'm about to head out. Take care of my girl?"

"Always." Wells gives her his signature megawatt smile. "I think she's almost ready to go home with you. What do you think?"

"That's what I said." I stand up and shut the door to Betty's little room. "But she wants to be out of her mom's house first. I gave her a perfectly acceptable offer, and she turned me down."

"For the record," Wells says, lookin' at River, "Rhett and I both told him it was too soon." His eyes move back to me. "Told you it was too soon."

"Y'all are both thorns in my ass." I throw an arm around River and kiss the side of her head. "But not you, darlin'. Let me walk you out."

CHAPTER TWENTY-SEVEN

River

I'M at work the next day, and I can't stop thinking about my conversation with Hayes. How he asked me to move in with him and how I chickened out *again* when it came to telling him about Addie's funeral. I wanted to say yes so badly. I wanted to run to my house, throw all of my crap into the Jeep, and drive as fast as possible back to his house.

But I know I can't do that until I come clean. I can't live with someone when there are still things we need to discuss. It was on the tip of my tongue when I was explaining how I'm working through my trust issues. It was so close to just falling out of my mouth, but fear ground everything to a halt.

He's going to be so pissed when he finds out I saw him in that state and still chose to go back to the city. I abandoned him, and I'm terrified for him to find out.

"I haven't seen you all freaking week!" Evie exclaims as she walks in the back door. "Our shifts keep missing, and you refuse to write anything down in a text message. So I am going to go put my shit up, and then you're gonna tell me all about your weeklong sexcapade."

I laugh and give her a mock salute. And after doing busy work for an hour while we go over every detail I'm willing to spill about Hayes and me, she's completely caught up on my love life.

"I told you he was going to show up like that, sweep you off your feet, and y'all would live happily ever after." She sighs and starts wiping down the counters. "Some people have all the luck."

"I don't think we are at the happily ever after yet." I smile at her. "We still have some stuff to work out."

"Don't let that little stuff get in the way of you being happy." She stops wiping and leans against her hip on the counter. "You were so quiet when you first came here. Granted, so was I," she says with a laugh. "But, I don't know, you just seemed sad a lot of the time. But ever since Hayes came back into your life? You've been so much happier. Lighter."

"That's so corny." I groan. "I'm like some little kid with a crush."

"Hey, River?" Dr. Martinez walks out of one of the exam rooms. "Can I chat with you for a minute when you're done?"

"Yeah, of course."

"And Evie, would you mind giving that one a nail trim?" She points with her thumb over her shoulder. "I won't keep River from you for long."

"No worries!" Evie runs off to the dog in the exam room, and I follow Martinez back to her office.

"Don't worry," she says as I sit down in front of her desk. "This isn't anything bad."

"Was the anxiety written all over my face?" I ask, laughing a little to push past the nerves.

"I am very accustomed to the feeling of being called into your boss's office. It's never a good feeling. But I actually just wanted to ask you about your future, what your plans are."

"Like, in general or…?"

"I guess, yeah." She shrugs. "I know you came back to Cane Creek to help your mom, but I wasn't sure if this was permanent or not."

I take a deep breath. Good question.

"I would like it to be," I tell her honestly. "I was a little done with the city anyway, and I love Cane Creek. I'm just trying to figure out a lot of stuff at the moment."

"I'm glad to hear you want to stay," she says with a smile. "Do you think this career path is what you'd like to stay on? Or do you see yourself doing something else?"

God, I feel like I'm twenty all over again, sitting in

my advisor's office, trying to pick my major. But now it's even worse because I'm almost thirty years old, and I should not be having this conversation. I should be past this by now.

"No, I've always wanted to work with animals. I don't want to be a vet," I tell her, laughing when I think about how much schooling you need for that. "Another four years for that doctorate? No, thank you."

"Completely understand," she says, laughing with me. "I love having you here. You're a hard worker, and you're great with the animals. So, I wanted to come to you with this first. I've been thinking about adding on to the business. I would like to add a self-wash and grooming business next door in the open lot."

"Oh, wow. That's a great idea!" We had a lot of the self-wash and grooming businesses in the city, and they were always packed when I'd walk by the one in my neighborhood. I think people like the idea of being able to wash their own dog without clogging their drains.

"I would like you to manage it."

I can feel my eyes go wide.

"Sorry?"

"I would like you to manage it." She's smiling at my shock. "I know it's not the same job you're in now, and I know you went to school to be a vet tech, so if you don't want to do this, that is totally understandable. But it will come with a big pay raise and a lot more freedom to make your own schedule."

"Oh, my god."

"Think about it." She leans back in her chair. "I'll give you the paperwork on it with your wage, tasks that will be expected of you, and anything else you might want to know about it before you leave. If you have any questions, let me know. Take some time."

I'm a little more than shocked. This is not something I saw coming, but as I walk out of her office, a wave of relief crashes over me. If this comes with a big enough pay bump, I won't have to work in the bar anymore. I could help Mom without killing myself in the process. And it would give me another reason to stay in town, live my life here with Hayes.

Pulling my phone out of my pocket, I send Hayes a quick text, telling him I have really big news. I can barely contain my excitement, and I want to tell him everything in a text. But it's too much, too big to put in a text. So I'm just going to have to wait another couple of hours. Barely a minute goes by before he's texting me back, telling me to come out for Saturday dinner before my shift at the bar.

"I need your help," Evie says, popping her head out of the exam room. "Stop smiling like a lovesick puppy, and come help me, please."

I laugh and shove my phone back into my pocket. I really want to tell Evie as well, hoping that maybe she'd want to work with me at the new business instead. Probably something I'd have to talk to Dr. Martinez about first, but Evie is always talking about how this job isn't where she wants to be for the rest of her life. So maybe running that new business with me is something that would interest her.

"So, what was all that about?" she asks once we're alone. She has the dog on the grooming table, but the poor thing is too fat to hold her back end up, making it impossible for Evie to get her back feet.

"Oh, nothing." I am a bad liar. "She was just telling me about some ideas she has."

"Alright, alright. Keep your secrets." Evie smiles up at me, not fazed at all that I haven't confided in her. "Hold her up for me, please?"

I nod and cradle the poor pup's hips.

CHAPTER TWENTY-EIGHT

Hayes

RIVER HAS the biggest smile on her face when she walks into the main house after she gets off work. Everyone is in the kitchen, and I meet her at the door as she kicks off her shoes.

"What's the big news, then, darlin'?" I ask as I lean in and kiss her on the cheek.

"Dr. Martinez wants to build on to the business," she tells me, the words rolling out of her in an excited tumble. She goes on to tell me all about their meeting and how the vet is interested in having River run the new business, coming with a big pay bump and better hours.

This is huge. I've been a little worried in the back of my mind lately, wondering if she was going to be happy here with working the jobs she has now. I knew she loved working at the vet's office, but with having to help her mom and support herself, she had to get a second job at the bar. And that was obviously never her end goal in life.

"So, you said yes, right?"

"She told me to take some time to think about it." She holds out a few sheets of paper, and I take them. "This is all the information on it. I guess it's the business proposal she took to the bank, explaining what she wants to do. And then on the back page," she says, flipping through the sheets, "that's the salary offer."

"Once again," I say, smiling at her, "you said yes, right? Because that's a damn good offer, baby."

"I have tomorrow off, and then I plan to talk to her on Monday. I mean, I should say yes, right? It would be stupid to turn that down!" Her eyes are bright with excitement. "I would get to spend my whole day with animals and have far better hours than I do now. And with that salary, I could stop working at the bar. No more late nights coming home smelling like booze and cigarettes."

"And I won't have to come to the bar every night to watch all those men fawn over you."

"No one asked you to do that." She smirks and walks past me. "In fact, I think I remember telling you that I get better tips when you aren't there."

"He scaring away all the good tippers?" Momma asks when she sees River walking into the kitchen. She and Poppy are working on finishing up the chicken, which smells fucking heavenly, and River fits right in between them.

"He is. I should have Bill ban him." She winks at me over her shoulder. "Now, what can I do to help you ladies?"

Dinner is delicious, and having River sit next to me the entire time, laughing and joking around with everyone like old times, makes me feel all warm and fuzzy inside. I can't stop watching her. I can barely keep up with what they're all talking about because all I do is listen to her laughter and watch the way her eyes sparkle.

She used to come over to dinners all the time when we were younger, choosing to eat with us instead of fending for herself at her own house. Janie was always gone, so River was here, eating and laughing with us every night. Back then, I think I was so caught up in how my family treated her like a daughter and a sister that I also just couldn't see her as anything else.

But seeing her fit in with us now, making conversation and giving to both Rhett and Wells just as good as she gets, I realize she was always meant to be here. River was always meant to be a sister to them, another daughter to my parents, and perfect for me. She could be all the things I saw her as when we were growing up together and still be something more to me today.

"Earth to Hayes," Wells says, snapping his fingers at

me from across the table. "Did you hear a lick of what we said?"

"What's up?" I look around the table and throw my arm on the back of River's chair. "What'd I miss?"

"Too busy ogling River," Poppy mumbles to Rhett.

"Heard that." I narrow my eyes at her, and she just laughs.

"I was telling them about the job offer, which led to me talking about the bar…" River looks nervous.

"And how you get to quit?" I wink at her.

"And how I got you a spot to perform on Thursday nights."

"What?" I look over at her, and her cheeks are turning the cutest shade of pink.

"Bill said you can have Thursday nights, and if you draw in a big enough crowd, he'll give you some time slots on the weekends." She shrugs, not meeting my eyes. "He actually sounded kind of put out that you had never asked him before."

"You did that for me?" My grin takes over my entire face because this is probably the nicest thing anyone has ever done for me.

She shrugs again.

"You love playing music, and you love living in this town. So why not combine the two?"

I grab her face and yank her over to me, planting a huge kiss right on her lips. Everyone's laughter mixes with Jo's and Wade's exaggerated gagging sounds.

"This family is becoming intolerable," Wells groans from across the table. "I have to be careful everywhere I go. You never know when you're gonna run into someone making out in a barn or gettin' it on in a field."

"Wells Black," Momma scolds. "Children are present."

"That's what I'm sayin'!" He laughs. "Children are present. We should all be mindful of that."

"I've gotta get going," River says as she begins to scoot back from the table. Poor girl is as red as a tomato. "My shift starts soon. Thank you so much for dinner."

"I'll walk you out." I stand with her.

"See you in a bit!" Poppy calls out after us.

"I'm so sorry," River whispers, her eyes wide with worry. "I don't know why I just blurted that out in front of your family like that. I was supposed to wait until we were alone and I could make sure you were okay with it first and—"

I kiss her to shut up her worrying thoughts.

"So, you're not upset, then?" Her eyes are heavy-lidded when she looks up at me.

"Not a bit."

"It just...came out. Like word vomit. And the second it did, my whole stomach dropped through the damn floor. Like, that was not how you were supposed to find out. I mean, shit...do you even want to perform anymore? I didn't even think about that!" Her eyes go even wider. "You can totally say no. Why didn't I think of all of these things before I asked Bill about this?"

"River." I take her face in both of my hands. "Hush. Stop spiraling. I promise you, I don't mind. What I do care about is you caring enough about me to go out of your way to do something nice for me." I kiss her again and again, little pecks all over her face until she's laughing and trying to pull away.

"Okay, okay!"

"You did a very nice thing for me, River Larson."

"So…you're excited?"

"I haven't played in front of people since I left the city. So while I'm excited, yes, I'm also a little nervous." I shrug. "You'll just have to help me work out that excess energy before the gig."

She throws her head back in laughter as I wag my eyebrows at her and squeeze a handful of ass. God, this woman drives me crazy in the best way possible.

"I have to go." She tries to disentangle herself from my arms, but I'm not willing to let her go yet.

"But I've barely had any time with you." I pull her back in, kiss her again, and try to lock in her sweet smell. "You should just quit. Stay here with me."

"Hayes." She erupts into a fit of giggles as she continues to fight my hold. "If I quit now, you might lose your gig."

"Screw the gig." I kiss her neck and love the way she kind of melts into me as she sighs.

"Don't get me all riled up before my shift." She groans when I tug on her ear with my teeth. "I don't want to be frustrated the entire night."

"But that's the fun part," I murmur against her throat. "The waiting. The anticipation."

"You say that now." She grabs my jaw and tugs it away from her neck. "I don't think you'll be saying it later when I get you back for this."

One of her dark eyebrows raises in a promise of what's to come, and that gets my dick's attention.

"Are you gonna play with me later, firefly?" My fingers flex against her ass. "Is that a promise?"

"Oh, it's a promise." She gives me a few gentle slaps on the cheek. "Now, let me go. I gotta go earn some tips."

I finally let her go and kneel in front of her when she sits down on the bench to put her boots back on. Being the gentleman that I am, I help her put them on, taking my time as I lace them up and tie them tightly. These combat boots are her favorite, and they've definitely seen better days.

"I don't know how to tie my shoes either." Wade walks through the living room to stand next to us. "It's complicated, and Daddy says since I wear my cowboy boots everywhere that it doesn't really matter." His little shoulders shrug as he watches me tie the final knot.

"No shame in that, my man," I tell him. "River is almost thirty and still can't do it."

River smacks me on the side of the head.

"Will you be at Uncle Hayes' in the morning?" Wade asks her.

"Possibly. Why? What's up?" She stands and collects her things.

"I'll see you tomorrow, then. Grammy always lets us bring everyone breakfast on Sunday mornin's. She says y'all need somethin' in your stomachs."

"I'll see you tomorrow morning, then. That's very sweet of you." River leans down and gives him a quick kiss on the head, then gives me the same treatment on my cheek. "See you later."

"Bye, darlin'." I smack her on her ass as she walks out the door.

CHAPTER TWENTY-NINE

River

ON SUNDAY MORNING, the kids and Katherine brought us breakfast. So, so much breakfast. They pulled up in one of their side-by-sides and pulled out two huge to-go plates of pancakes, bacon, eggs, and a pitcher of orange juice. I was eating until my stomach was too full to move.

The rest of the day was spent lying around with Hayes, watching our favorite movies and eating junk food. I baked cookies for him, and he gave me a massage that didn't lead to sex. Well, right away anyway.

And then Monday, I walked into Dr. Martinez's office and accepted her offer. I also asked her about Evie helping me out, and she was all for it as long as we could find replacements for both of us at the vet's office.

They're slated to break ground on the new place within the next couple of weeks, which means I'll have a brand-new job by Thanksgiving. It finally feels like everything is falling into place, and I can suddenly *breathe* again. I'm honestly just waiting for the other shoe to drop because between Hayes, my job, and loving my life in this little town again, it's all too good to be true.

Which reminds me, I still haven't told Hayes about me coming back for Addie's funeral. I keep waking up thinking that today is the day, and then he turns over and pulls me into his chest, holding me tight while we both slowly wake up together, and I just can't do it.

So I tell myself I'll do it after work, when we're eating dinner or sitting outside on the porch. But then I feel like we're so happy, and we've both had long days. That's not the time to do it either. And Poppy keeps pestering me about it. Every day I show up to see Betty, and Poppy will ask me if I've told him yet, like holding out on him is my one fatal flaw.

Which, maybe it is. But it's like the longer I go without telling him, the more I think maybe I don't have to. Or I just *can't*. It's like when I was in school and I knew I had a paper due. We would know weeks in advance that the research paper had to be done, but I would think I had plenty of time. So a few days would go by, and then a week, and then another.

And I just kept thinking it would be fine. No biggie.

I procrastinate all the time, so *surely* I had enough time to finish the paper. But then we'd get a reminder three days out, and I would have to literally cram weeks' worth of research and writing into seventy-two hours.

Which is what I'm doing here. I keep putting it off and putting it off. And there's going to be a day where it comes up or he brings it up, and I'm going to have to admit this horrible thing I've done to him. Then, because I've waited so long, it's going to be even worse. He's going to blow up about how long I've been hiding this from him, and it'll be so, so much worse.

I take a deep breath. I'm spiraling, and it's gotta stop.

Leaning back against the outside of the bar, I wait for Hayes and his family to get here. I'm working tonight, but it's slower than a weekend, so I'm able to take longer breaks. And Bill knows that Hayes and I are friends, which means he'll let me watch the gig and slack off a little tonight to support him.

A couple of trucks pull in, and the gravel crunches as they make their way over to the front of the bar. The entire family pours out, all smiles and excited energy. I've missed this family so much, and I feel like I've fit back into my old spot with ease. Katherine and Clyde treat me like a daughter again, and Rhett and Wells have taken to teasing me just like they used to.

And Poppy has become a really good friend, and I kind of hope we can be sisters someday. Once she and

Rhett tie the knot, maybe Hayes and I will, too, eventually.

Speak of the devil. There's my man, walking across the parking lot with his guitar slung over his back and his baseball cap on backward, causing his hair to stick out the sides. He never used to keep it this long, but I love it. I like giving those soft stands a good tug when he's between my thighs.

"Hey there, darlin'." The ghost of a dimple appears on his cheek, and I can feel my heart kick up a beat.

"Hi." He leans down and kisses me. "Nervous?"

"A bit." He shrugs. "But mostly excited."

"We'll go in and get a table, son," Clyde says, giving him a rough squeeze on the shoulder. He turns to me and winks. "You help him calm down so he doesn't blow it up there."

"But don't blow him," Wells whispers as he walks past, following the rest of his family inside. "We're in public."

"Wells!" I cry out, slapping him hard on the arm and sending him stumbling to the side. "Watch your mouth."

He's laughing his ass off as he walks inside, but Hayes steals back my attention, putting both of his hands on either side of my head and surrounding me with his woodsy cologne. He rarely wears it, but every time he does, I soak it up.

"You look beautiful," he says, his voice low and warm. "You wear that pretty little dress for me, firefly?"

"This old thing?" I tease. "Maybe." I did pick it out just for him. It's a short red summer dress with little white flowers all over it. It's strappy but with a high neck so I don't accidentally flash any of the patrons. That's the last thing I need — Hayes killing someone for seeing my tits.

"Easy access," he says, running one of his hands up my thigh. That slightest touch makes my panties wet. I kind of like how he's touching me when anyone could walk out and catch us. He gets impossibly closer, his scruff scratching against my cheek. "Gonna let me throw it over your hips later while I have you bent over the bed?"

"Maybe," I drawl. "But Wells gave me a little idea."

I smirk up at him as his eyebrows draw together.

"I don't like hearing my brother's name on your lips while we're this close, River. Not one bit."

I laugh and grab hold of his hand, tugging him around the side of the building. The sun is setting, but it's still high enough that it feels like we're doing this in the middle of the afternoon. Once we're out of sight of the parking lot, I lift his guitar over his head and give him a firm shove against the wood siding.

"Ooh, feisty." He wags his eyebrows. "What're we doin' back here?"

As an answer, I lean his guitar against the wall as

well and then run my hands down the front of his shirt. I can feel the hard muscles of his abs jump and flex under my palms until they rest on the button of his jeans.

"River?" He looks from me to where my hands are and back. "What are you doin', woman?"

"I'm going to help you take the edge off."

I unbutton his jeans and sink down to my knees as I pull down his zipper. His breathing picks up, and I can already see he's getting hard. So responsive for me.

"River Larson." He groans as my hand slips inside the fly of his boxers and tugs his hardening cock out. "We could get caught."

"Oh, hush." I grip him at the base and give it one firm stroke. "If you're fast enough, no one will even miss us."

Without waiting for him to agree, I lick him from base to tip, and he's suddenly very long and hard in my hand. And when I circle my tongue around his head and suck him into my mouth, a very long line of inappropriate language cascades out of his mouth. His fingers tangle in my hair, and I look up at him from under my lashes, relishing the way he's looking down at me.

He looks at me like he loves me, and that only spurs me on. As he looks around to make sure we're actually alone, I take him deeper. I've been practicing with his length, trying to get him deeper and deeper until he's fully inside of my throat. And this time, it happens. The moment my nose touches the soft hair at his base, he moans, and his toes must curl because he goes high up on his tiptoes.

"Jesus fucking *Christ*, River." He pulls me off and looks down at me. "You tryin' to make me cross-eyed?"

"Just trying to make you come, baby." I take him back in my mouth, working him with both my fist and my mouth a few more times before I pop back off. "So relax and let it happen. You've got a gig to play and a family that's waiting for you."

"Shit."

His hands never leave my hair, but he stops trying to tug me off him. Instead, he takes control, his hands moving my head in time with the flexing of his hips. The gravel bites into my knees, and my clit is throbbing. It's going to be hard as hell to go back to work after this without getting off.

"That's it, baby."

He's whispering, barely coherent as he praises me over and over again, pushing himself deeper and deeper down my throat. Drool begins to run past my lips and down my chin, and my eyes are watering as I struggle to catch my breath in between pumps.

"I'm gonna come, River." He's panting. "Can you swallow for me, baby?"

He looks down at me and strokes my chin with his fingers.

"Swallow all of it for me, okay?"

I moan and try to nod, but he gets what I'm trying to

say. He watches me through his entire orgasm, and I swallow over and over again as he finishes. His mouth hangs open slightly, and his eyes roll back for a moment. And then he's done, sliding out of my mouth and tucking himself away as I wipe the sides of my mouth.

"My god." He squats down and lifts me up onto my feet, taking a moment to brush the little pebbles out of the skin on my knees. "You're fucking perfect."

He kisses me, tasting himself on my tongue as he dives deep into my mouth, kissing me senseless.

"Feel better?" I ask him, grinning when he blows out a puff of air.

"I'd sure as shit hope so." He tries to fix my hair with his fingers. "But I'm tellin' you, the second we walk in there, everyone is gonna know what we've been up to. Between your poor knees and how red your lips are."

I shrug.

"That's all part of the fun, isn't it?"

He shakes his head and grins.

"Where'd you come from, firefly?"

"Been here this whole time, handsome." I reach around and smack his ass. "Now, go play some damn guitar."

CHAPTER THIRTY

Hayes

THE GIG WENT REALLY WELL. There was a relatively big turnout. Granted, a decent number of those people turned out to be women that I used to be involved with…but whatever. It still felt good to be up in front of people doin' something I enjoy again. And getting to do it for the first time in front of River? Priceless.

I kept finding her throughout my whole set, and each time, she was watching me with a big smile on her face. It's pretty incredible what lookin' at her does for my confidence. Her smile just makes me soar.

And makes me hard. Because when her pretty pink lips stretch into a big ole smile, I can't help but think about what that mouth was doing before the show. Christ, how did I get so lucky? My girl dropped to her knees and took me deep into her throat without a second thought and looked damn good doing it.

That's what I'm thinking about when I step off the small, raised stage. I'm ready to get back to my usual spot at the bar, where I can keep an eye on her for the rest of her shift. But I'm stopped and bombarded by a flock of women, all smiling too sweetly and smelling of sickly perfume. God, it's like they all bathed in it to make sure it would burn through my nose hair.

My most recent ex, Ashley, speaks first, her red hair twirled around her finger.

"You were great!"

"Thank you." I give her a polite smile and then glance back up toward the bar. River is staring her down like she's hoping her gaze can light her on fire.

And then, like a well-oiled machine, they all take turns complimenting me and trying to make small talk. But I can't focus on anything except the jealous look in River's eyes. It's doin' something for me.

"Haven't really seen you around much," Ashley says, stepping a bit closer and nudging the other girls out of the way. They take the hint, I guess, and slowly dissipate, leaving Ashley and me alone.

"Been right here."

"Well, I haven't seen you." She puts on a pout. "And I've wanted to. I think it's a shame the way we ended things."

"With you throwin' a full cup of coffee across your kitchen at my head?"

She shrugs and tries to smile seductively at me. It just makes me grimace.

"I have a little bit of a temper." Her voice gets lower, and she steps even closer. I feel like I can barely breathe; the scent of her is cloying. "But if I remember correctly, you seemed to like that when it came to the bedroom."

I throw my head back with a loud laugh.

"Not gonna happen," I tell her, shaking my head. "Never going to happen, ever again."

"Oh, come on, Hayes." Her hand comes out and runs down the front of my shirt. "Why not?"

"Ashley," I say, grabbing her hand and removing it from my body. "I won't hit a woman. But you see that pretty lady back there?"

I point over her shoulder at River, who is staring daggers at us as she dries a glass.

"She will."

As if River heard me, she sets the glass down, throws the towel on the bar, and starts marching over toward us. My woman is on a mission, making it across the bar in record time. I just lean back against the wall and smile at her.

River fists my shirt, completely ignoring Ashley, and yanks me down to her height as she kisses me hard. There's the fire I was waitin' for. My hands immediately sink into her hair as our tongues dance together. This little act of her claiming me in public, just like I did to her in the restaurant, is making me hard as stone.

"You ever let another woman touch you again, Hayes Black, and I will use my teeth before your next gig."

"Yes, ma'am." I grin down at her.

"River," Ashley says while looking down her nose at her. "Just had to snatch Hayes right back up the moment you're in town?"

"Ashley." River mocks her tone. "Just had to touch what isn't yours the moment you realize it didn't want you anymore?"

"I resent being called an *it*," I grumble behind her.

"You'll be perfect together." Ashley sneers at me when I wrap an arm around River's shoulders and pull her back into my front. "You're both just the epitome of class."

"Careful, Ashley," River warns. "Use big words and your brain might overheat."

For a second, I'm worried that Ashley is going to get her claws out and use them on River's face. I tense, ready to pull her out of the way if Ashley decides she's going to lash out. I'm familiar with the look. Hell, her throwin' that coffee mug at me wasn't the first time she chucked something at me. It was the first time she hit her target, though. I had a black eye for a week.

"Whatever." Ashley whips around, her hair almost

smacking River in the face, and stalks off back to her group of women. She says something, and within a few minutes, they're all following her out the front door.

"I need you to stand here for a second," I whisper into River's ear. "Because that little display of jealousy has my cock about to burst through my zipper."

"I was so ready to watch a fight," Wells says, walking over with Rhett and Poppy.

"I was ready to give backup." Poppy holds her fists up like she's ready to fight, bouncing on her toes like a boxer.

"Easy, killer." Rhett rolls his eyes and gently pushes her arms down with a soft smile. He looks at her like she's the sun he revolves around, and I wonder if that's what I look like when I look at River.

"See you kids back at home." Momma smiles as she walks up to me and gives me a kiss on the cheek. "You did fantastic, baby."

"Thanks, Momma."

"Proud of you, son." Pops claps me on the shoulder. "Good to see you so happy."

River cranes her head back to look at me as my parents walk away, and I kiss her on her forehead. I know why I look so happy, and it's not just because I'm playing in front of people again. It's because of this girl right here in my arms and the way she gave me a second chance.

"We're gonna head out. Babysitter couldn't stay late

tonight." Rhett gives me one of his rare smiles. "You did good, Hayes."

"Careful. Y'all are gonna give him a praise kink with all this mushy shit," Wells jokes. "And then he'll be insufferable."

"He already is most of the time," River chimes in.

"I didn't realize it was rip on Hayes hour?"

Everyone has a good little laugh at my expense and then says their goodbyes. I'll get a ride home with River after her shift, and I have Rhett take my guitar so I don't have to carry it around for the rest of the night. River is on a closing shift with Bill and another bartender tonight, so we'll be here for a while.

But when we get to the bar, Bill tells us to leave for the night, that he and the other girl can handle it.

"You've been working a lot of shifts," he tells her. "Take the night off and have some fun."

"Are you sure?" She seems hesitant to accept the night off. But I'm not.

"He's sure," I answer for him, smiling when he rolls his eyes at me. We've all known Bill since we were kids, and he's a good guy. "Let's go."

"You treat her right, Hayes Black!" he calls out as I walk her out of the bar. "She's a good one."

"She's a great one," I tell him. Probably *the* one, I think to myself.

CHAPTER THIRTY-ØNE

Hayes

"CAN I DRIVE?" I ask as we walk over to her Jeep.

"I suppose?" She gives me a questioning look. "Why?"

"Because I have somewhere I want to take you."

She tosses me the keys.

"Is this where you take me to some secluded spot and murder me? Dump my body somewhere no one will ever find me?"

I give her a look. "You are listening to way too many serial killer podcasts."

"They're good to fall asleep to."

"You're off your rocker." I take her hand after we're on the road. "I kind of liked what I saw in there."

She blushes.

"I don't know what came over me. I've never let

jealousy take over like that. But when I saw her touch you?" She blows out a huff of air. "All bets were off."

"I was ready for you to slap her." I wink over at her as she groans and laughs.

"I would've for sure lost my job then."

"Nah. Bill's known me since I was a kid. He'd keep you around if I vouched for you." I bring her hand to my lips and kiss her knuckles. "It was hot, baby. Stop worrying about it. Got me hard."

"Yeah?" She looks over at me like I've kind of lost my mind. "Jealousy and violence get you going?"

"Anything and everything about you gets me goin', firefly."

I really like making her blush.

The drive to the bird sanctuary is a good clip out into the country, and it's pitch-black by the time I pull into the long dirt road that leads to the entrance. It's part of a state park that is hardly ever monitored. I used to come out here when River was gone, Dean was off the wagon, and I needed a moment to think.

There's hardly any light pollution out here, so the night sky is lit up like crazy. You can see the cloudy formation of the Milky Way and all the constellations you could ever hope to see on this side of the globe. It's pretty fucking romantic if you ask me.

"What is this place?" she asks as we finally pull up to the gravel parking lot.

"Technically, for bird-watching," I tell her. "It's part of a protected piece of land with the state, but I swear no one hardly knows about it."

"How'd you find it?" She steps out of the Jeep and smiles up at the sky with excited eyes.

"Can't remember, honestly." I shrug and join her, taking her hand to lead her through the trail. "I think I was just driving around, trying to get lost on back roads. Came across this, and it was deserted. So it kind of became my special little spot."

"Trying to get lost on back roads? In this backcountry? Good way to end up shot, Hayes."

"Please," I groan. "You sound like Momma. These old ranchers ask questions first, then shoot."

She laughs and rolls her eyes.

"So, where are you taking me? It's kind of creepy out here. Are you sure you aren't bringing me out here to kill me?"

It is creepy. Especially the first time I came out here by myself. The grass is tall, about as tall as River, and it's eerily quiet. Makes you feel like anyone — or anything — could be lurking out there. And when the wind blows and the grass rustles, it can make the hair on the back of your neck stand on end.

"I've been out here many times," I tell her. "Never had any issue or run into another person. It's just creepy because it's so quiet. There's a big-ass platform that will come into view in a sec. We're gonna go out there and stargaze for a bit."

"Cute," she says, bumping into me as we walk on the dirt path.

Eventually, the wooden platform comes into view, and we make our way over to it. It's about a story high, and the old wood creaks under our weight as we climb up the stairs.

"I've never brought anyone out here," I tell her as we sit and lie back on the wood planks. "My family doesn't even know about this place."

"Thank you." She takes my hand and brings it to her lips. "This is insane. I mean, you have amazing skies at the ranch, but this is next-level."

"I used to come out here when I was hung up on what happened with us." I stare up at the night sky. "I've gone over and over that fight so many times. I've changed the things I said and the way I just let you leave. I've daydreamed about driving back to Bozeman to find you again, and instead of leaving, I would talk to you until you would listen. I'd bring you back home and never let you walk away again."

"That's kidnapping," she teases. "Sorry, didn't mean to make a joke of it."

"No, it's fine." I smile over at her. "I was a sad sack

for a while when you were gone. You kind of brought the light back when you showed up."

"I used to do that, too, ya know," she tells me. "I'd lay in bed at night wondering what we could've done differently. More specifically, what *you* could've done differently."

We both laugh, even though it's not really that funny. God, I was an ass.

"Calling you easy was *not* the move." I regret everything I said in that fight, but that one really takes the cake.

"No it was not." She rolls onto her side and wraps an arm around me. "But you've changed. I can see it all the time. In the way you show up every day, helping me with Betty and making sure I'm taken care of when I stay over at your place. You've become this incredibly giving person, Hayes. You're still the same man I knew as a kid, just grown up."

"You've not changed at all," I tell her, laughing when her face is shocked. "It's a good thing! You didn't lose any of that spark that made you *you*. You're still fiery, and you love hard. You're still kind, compassionate, and empathetic."

She leans forward and runs her fingers through my hair for a moment before kissing me. I'm a lost cause when it comes to this woman. I drown in her and love every goddamn second of it. I wrap her up in my arms and roll her onto her back.

"I owe you," I murmur against her mouth. "Since I'm such a giving person and all."

She laughs as my lips move down her throat, kissing and tasting every inch I can get my hands on. Her knees fall open as I settle between them, and her soft hands run up and down my arms. She's always talking about my biceps and the way my veins show on my forearms. Never thought veins would be a thing that's considered attractive, but she's always running her fingers over them, tracing their paths.

I push her dress up over her hips and then her breasts and tug down the soft fabric of her bra. They're such a perfect, soft handful with hard, pointed nipples. I take one in my mouth, and she moans and lifts her hips in response. My cock is already hard again, begging to be set free. But this is about her, giving back for what she did for me before the gig.

I tug off her tight little shorts she's wearing, along with her underwear, and then kiss the soft skin of her stomach all the way down to where she wants me. When I look up, those gorgeous blue eyes are locked on what I'm doing. I love the way she likes to watch.

"How wet are you, River?" Using my thumbs, I spread her wide and then blow cool air across her swollen clit. She is glistening with arousal, and it makes my mouth water. "All for me, baby?"

"Yes," she says on an exhale.

There is nothing like tasting my woman. And in the

quiet of this special spot, I eat her like a starving man. I suck and lick and suck and lick, pushing her closer and closer to the edge with each swipe. Her hips jerk and roll against my face, and I have to wrap my arms around her hips to keep her steady.

She's soon panting my name and praising me. Shit, maybe I do have a praise kink.

"Fuck, you're so good at that." She moans and grabs hold of my hair. "So fucking good, Hayes. You know just what I like, don't you?"

I nod as I continue my task, and within a few more minutes, her body is tensing as she cries out through her orgasm. She soaks my chin, and I don't stop, slowly licking and tasting until she comes down and becomes a bit too sensitive. I kiss her inner thighs and then grab her underthings and slip them back on.

Once she's put back together, she lies there like a starfish, breathing deeply with her eyes closed.

"You are truly stunning. You know that, firefly?" I lie down next to her and pull her into my arms. She curls up, fitting into my side like she belongs there.

"Thank you for bringing me here," she says, her voice quiet and tired. "It's beautiful. And I like being in a spot that has so much of you in it. Feels like you're really bringing me back into your life."

"Wouldn't have it any other way, darlin'." I kiss the top of her head and sigh. "Wouldn't have it any other way."

CHAPTER THIRTY-TWO

River

"SO WHEN DOES this new job start?" Poppy asks as I help her clean out the dogs' stalls.

"They just broke ground on it this week, so depending on how long the build takes with weather and such, probably before Thanksgiving."

"How excited are you?"

"Pretty freaking excited. I told her about how you used to work at a boarding and daycare place, and she asked if I could steal you from the ranch to help out." I laugh.

"I would love to help!" She closes one of the gates and leans against the wall. "Not sure when I would have the time, but I would be more than happy to pop in on my days off for a few hours."

"That's ridiculous. Don't offer her that," I tell her.

"She will snatch you up, and Wells would never forgive me."

"Fine." She rolls her eyes. "But the offer to you stands. Just let me know. Was Hayes excited for you?"

"Very." I smile. "I think he was worried about how long I would actually stick around working two jobs."

"He'd follow you to Bozeman if you asked him."

"He would." I finish cleaning the last bit of the stall and then close the gate. "But that's not where I want to be. And I don't want him leaving the ranch when this place needs the help."

"I'm hoping once Dean comes back things will ease up a little." She closes her eyes and leans her head back. "Rhett is so stressed about money because so much of it is going to Dean's treatment. Once that's freed up, maybe we can actually hire on some people."

"Has he said how many he needs?" I ask her. "I remember when I was a kid, this place probably had double the amount of people working on it. I'm surprised it's still keeping its head above water."

"He hasn't said. But I know he needs a lot of help. He keeps saying just a couple more months before Dean is out, and things should get better." She shrugs and looks back over at me. "I know it'll be fine. He won't let this place go under, but it doesn't mean he isn't stressed as hell about it.

"And," she continues, "we have more animals coming this week."

"How many?"

"Few dogs, a couple cats that will be fixed and made into barn cats, and some livestock. I think he said he's got a couple of horses coming, too."

"Why does he keep taking them in? Surely he could just put a pause to the rescue side of things for a while until he gets his feet back under him."

"He could. But that, to him, is like letting Addie down." She shrugs. "And he won't do that."

Talk of Addie makes my chest hurt. Every time she gets brought up, I can feel the stress of keeping this secret from Hayes just wrap around my stomach like a vise grip. I'm so tired of being anxious all the time. I have to man up and spit it out.

Betty comes up to me, nudging my leg with her nose. She's out walking around on her long lead. We put a stake in the middle of the barn to start letting her get used to bigger spaces, and she's really taken to it. Her tail wags, and she sniffs every little scent she can find. We've slowly introduced other dogs to her one day at a time, and she's not once acted aggressively.

She's less skittish and seems to warm up to people much faster than she had been. Even the kids have been back — heavily supervised — and she lets them love all over her. It's finally looking like she's ready to come home with me. I'm just not sure which home that's going to be.

I've been staying at Hayes' house every night, only

going home to get clothes when I need them. Mom has noticed but doesn't really care as long as the money is still coming in. The creditors are slowly backing off, and getting those bills down is finally taking some weight off my shoulders. But thinking about taking Betty there, setting her up to live in that house… I just don't like it.

I'm not sure I trust Mom to be around her when I can't be there. I'll be able to take Betty into work with me at the vet's office, but once I go to the bar, she'll have to stay home. And Mom has never been an animal person. On top of that, she's too depressed to even care about her own daughter, so there's no way she's going to take care of a dog.

But I know that I can't take her to Hayes'. Not yet.

"Hey, baby girl." I squat down and give her kisses. "Are you enjoying your new freedom?"

"Think you might take her with you soon?" Poppy asks hopefully.

"Soon." I sigh. "I just—"

"Need to have a conversation with Hayes," she finishes for me.

I nod.

"I'm not pushing you to do anything you aren't ready for. I'm really not, River." She reaches out and puts a hand on my shoulder. "But the longer you wait, the harder it's going to get."

"I should've just told him when we first hashed

things out. When he was apologizing to me, I should've taken my turn." Something catches Betty's nose, and she trots off in search of it. I stand back up and rest my head against the wall. "But I was too caught up in being friends with him again and just wanting to be around him that I couldn't make myself speak."

"You know, Rhett told me Hayes brought it up."

"When?" My stomach falls through the floor, my gut twisting and turning.

"He said they were talking about it that morning when you came over while they built the deck. Hayes had told them he was head over heels but that there was just something in the back of his mind bugging him about how you never showed up for Addie."

"Shit."

"He blames himself, you know." Her smile is sad. "He thinks that he made you feel so much hatred for him and made you feel so uncomfortable that you couldn't even bear to come home for her funeral."

Fuck.

That pulls my heart out of my chest and stomps on it.

"I didn't know…"

"Well." She sighs. "He doesn't know either, River. He doesn't know that your mom was too caught up in her own life to tell you. He doesn't know that you were willing to forget about what happened between you guys for a little bit to be there for him. He's still under the impression you hated him."

"I know, I know." I groan and slide down the wall until I'm hugging my knees to my chest. "I'm a shitty person. I know."

"You are *not* a shitty person, River Larson." She sits next to me on the floor and takes my hands in her own. "You've both been through a lot. And anyone who says otherwise doesn't understand what it's like to go through the heartache you went through. That shit changes a person. You were scared. You had responsibilities back at school. You didn't leave him out of spite or to purposefully make him suffer."

"I left him alone." My voice breaks, even though I'm whispering.

"He was not alone." Her voice is firm and sure as she scoots closer. "He had his whole family. And I'm not blaming him at all, but you were alone, too, River. You went back to the city, and you had to heal from the grief of losing Addie alone. You didn't even know she was that sick…you didn't get to say goodbye."

I choke back a sob.

"Grief is messy," she continues. "Losing someone you love causes a deep ache that never really goes away. Hell, it barely lessens as time goes on. And it sucks that you didn't have one another when you needed each other. It really does. But you guys have to stop throwing blame around like you are."

I take a deep breath and try to center myself.

"You can't keep hiding this from him," she says. "It's going to eat you alive. And eventually, it'll come out. His parents will say something, or Rhett or Wells will. He's going to feel betrayed if that happens. If he doesn't hear it from you first, that shit is going to sting."

We both hear the footsteps at the same time, and I wipe my eyes as I straighten up, and Poppy moves away from me a touch. Hayes walks around the side of the barn and leans against the doorframe. The way he's looking at me…I feel like I'm going to throw up.

"Poppy." He nods in her direction, and she says hello before going back to cleaning up. Hayes turns toward me, his eyes cold and sad at the same time. "Care to have a chat?"

CHAPTER THIRTY-THREE

Hayes

I DIDN'T MEAN to eavesdrop. But when I heard Poppy talking and River sniffling, something in my gut just told me to stay put, to give them their privacy for a minute. I had been workin' hard all goddamn morning to get off in time to see River before she went to the bar. She didn't know I was going to make it over here today, but I wanted to see her.

And then I heard it. I heard her call herself a shitty person. I heard her say how she left me all alone. I heard Poppy say that she went *back* to the city. Which means River was here. River showed up for Addie and then left without a single word to me or my family.

That little spot in the back of my brain that's been telling me something was wrong…turns out it was right.

"Did you hear everything, then?" Her voice is small

and quiet. She's barely looking at me as we walk out into the nearby field.

"I don't know, River. You tell me."

We come to a stop next to the fence, and she tries to look anywhere but at me. She's chewing on her lips, and her arms are crossed over her chest. She looks like a kid who got in trouble at school and now has to tell their parents all about it. Meanwhile, I'm trying my hardest not to fall apart. My gut reaction is to scream or walk away without letting her explain.

But there's a part of me that feels like I owe her this. I asked her to stop runnin' from me, and I promised myself I'd never react like I did all those years ago. So, I'm trying. I am trying to stand here and listen to her, get the facts straight, instead of lashing out.

"I didn't know Addie was sick," she starts. "I mean, I knew she was sick, obviously. She was sick her whole life. But I didn't know she was *that* sick. I was walking out of a final, where I obviously had my phone turned off. And when I turned it back on, I had a missed call from Mom about twenty minutes before. Alarm bells started going off because Mom never calls me. Ever.

"I called her back three goddamn times before she picked up the phone. She sounded…bored. Like she couldn't care less that Addie had died or that my best friend had just lost his sister. She was just calling to tell me about the funeral, and how pretty it was, and how sad everyone seemed that I wasn't there."

She sniffs and coughs, and as she's wiping her eyes, it takes all the restraint I have not to pull her into my chest and wipe those tears away from her. But my mind and heart are raging at each other right now, confused and hurt, and I have no clue what to do as she stands here and confesses this secret she's been holding on to.

"It was late afternoon at this point," she tells me. "I ran across campus, jumped in a taxi, and went straight home. I think I blacked out in sheer panic and grief. I was throwing whatever clothes were on hand into a duffel bag and left. I drove *straight* here, Hayes."

The tears are flowing steadily now, making her blue eyes look darker. She reaches out for me, and as a gut reaction, I take a step back. I regret it, but I can't have her touching me right now. I just can't. Not when I know where this is going. Not when I know she abandoned me.

"I pulled into the driveway on two wheels and ran out of my car. I didn't even knock on your parents' door. The lights were on inside, so I just…barged in. It was late, but everyone was up, gathered around the fire in the living room. I was a blubbering mess, apologizing over and over again for not being there, for their loss."

"And then you left?" I ask her. "Just thought, oh, fuck Hayes. He'll be fine."

"No!" she cries out and goes to grab me again, but I step away. "Not at all. I was asking about you, but everyone said you had run off after the funeral."

Christ, did I? I guess I did. I don't remember a lot from that first week we lost her. I was too drunk to care about anything but the grief I was processing. Or trying to process. My poor liver probably wanted to kill me. But I just can't imagine not remembering River showing up. That seems huge. Sure, I had dreams about her. Drunken dreams that started with me begging for her forgiveness and ended with her in my arms as we cried together.

"I came to find you." Her voice has gone soft again, and she's finally really looking at me. "They said you were at Bill's bar and that Rhett and Wells had tried to get you to come home, but you wouldn't budge. Too stubborn, drunk, and sad to be coherent. When I found you, you were slumped against the wall outside, head hung over. You were passed out cold next to a pile of vomit.

"I slapped you around a bit to wake you up, and we somehow managed to get you in my Jeep. Only had to stop twice for you to vomit." She tries to laugh. "Anyway, your brothers and your dad got you set up in bed."

"And then you left." I spit it out like venom.

"I thought you wouldn't want me to see you like that." She shrugs, and a small sob escapes her. "You were so mad at me that day..."

"Don't!" I don't raise my voice. I don't yell at her. But I put even more distance between us and speak firmly. "You do *not* get to blame a stupid little fight we had as the reason you left me and my family when my fucking sister died. I had come to terms with me pushing you away so hard that you couldn't even come back to town. But to come back, see me in that state, and *still* leave? I can't make that work in my head, River."

"Hayes." Another sob. "Please, I just…I didn't think you would want me to see you like that. I didn't think you would want me there. And I had exams that I couldn't miss. I *had* to go back to Bozeman."

"But you stayed away, River." I take my hat off, run my hands through my hair as I pace in a circle, and then shove it back on my head. "You could've come back. You could've come back when finals were done. You could've explained everything and been there. But you *abandoned* me.

"Hell," I continue. "You could've told me once we started talking again. Once we were friends again. You could've told me before I kissed you, before I fucked you. Before I asked you to move in with me!"

She flinches at my words, and I know I'm being too harsh, but I can't stop it. I can't make my mouth shut the fuck up.

"You could've told me so many times, River. And you chose not to. You chose to tell Poppy but not me. It was a conscious decision to hide this from me."

"Did you stop to wonder why?" She throws her hands up at her sides. "Have you thought for a second here that maybe I hid this from you because I was afraid of this reaction? That I was afraid to lose you all over again?"

I put my hands on my hips and turn away from her. I can't look at the anguish that's so clearly written all over her face.

"And did it occur to you, Hayes, that I'm not the only one that hid this from you?"

Of course it did. I listened. I heard her story. I heard her tell me that my parents and my brothers both knew that she had come and just chose to never tell me. Even when I was talking to Rhett and Wells about it the other week, they both remained silent. When I was worried about it, when it was stuck in the back of my brain like a fuckin' parasite trying to eat away at the happiness I had with her.

Everyone kept this from me.

"Please don't shut down." The tears are falling faster now when I turn back around. "Just talk to me, Hayes. I'm so sorry. I should've stayed. I should've been there for you, and I let stupid shit get in the way. I'm so sorry."

"I can't." I reach out and pull her into a hug as she shakes and cries. My shirt gets soaked within a matter of seconds as I hold her tightly. "I can't talk this out with you right now, River."

Her arms tighten around my torso, and she cries harder. My heart is breaking, fucking shattering into a million pieces hearing her cry like this. But I need a minute. I need time to myself to sort through all of my thoughts and emotions. If I want to make this work, if I don't want to fuck it all up like I did over ten years ago, then I need some time alone. I need to get my fucking head straight.

"Please," she begs. "Please don't leave me again."

I take her face in my hands and make her look at me. Her poor cheeks are red and blotchy, and her tears have completely soaked her face. When she looks up at me, I try to help her breathe.

"Breathe with me, firefly." In and out. In and out. "Breathe."

She sniffs and tries her hardest to calm down, her tears slowing and her breaths evening out.

"I'm not sayin' this is over, okay? I'm just sayin' that I need some time." I kiss the top of her head as she sinks back into my arms, crying just as hard as before. "I have to go, River."

She cries harder, her arms squeezing the life out of me as I try to slip from her grasp. If I stay here any longer, I'm going to cave. If I cave, I'm going to resent her. I *have* to work through the thoughts and emotions going through my mind right now, or we will never be fully us again.

"River, please." My own voice cracks as her tears get to me. I can't fucking do this. "I have to go, baby. Just give me some time."

"If I let you walk away, you won't come back!" she cries into my chest.

"Hey!" Poppy comes running out of the barn. "River, come with me, babe."

"I just need some time." My eyes are pleading with Poppy to understand and help me. But she won't look at me.

"Come on, honey." Poppy finally peels her away from me, and River collapses into her. "Let's go back inside, okay? Betty will give you some love."

"I'm sorry," I whisper. "I just—"

"Hayes," Poppy says, looking over her shoulder as she helps River walk back to the barn. "Just go. I have her."

"I—"

"*I have her*," she says again. "Go."

So I do.

CHAPTER THIRTY-FOUR

River

IT'S PRETTY wild how one event can give you perspective on so many other things in your life. I've been lying in bed for the past three days, going over everything that got me to this point. No one wants to be twenty-eight, single, and living in their mom's house. So I've just been trying to figure out where I went wrong.

"You're not single," Poppy had said as I dried my tears on the floor of the barn. "He did not break up with you. He just said he needed some time."

Still feel single. The look of betrayal on his face is burned into my brain. I should've told him. Why didn't I just tell him? Or stay? I should've stayed. I should've emailed my professors and told them what happened. People get to make up tests all the time. I just used those finals as an excuse to get the hell out of Dodge. I was too selfish to stick around.

And now it feels like he's left me all over again. My dad left me when he died. My mom left me mentally when Dad passed. Janie even left me to go live in New York and get married. Hayes essentially left me twelve years ago. Addie…

Everyone leaves. Everyone always leaves.

I roll over and cry into my pillow, wanting to scream from the amount of hurt I feel over all of it. He told me to stop running. I did. And look where it got me.

There's a knock at my door. Oh, lovely. Mom has decided to notice me for once.

"Yeah?"

She says nothing, just opens the door, walks over to my bed, and sits on the edge. I roll back over and look at her. She's so frail now, her body just wasting away a day at a time. Janie and I tried to get her to go to therapy. We knew she needed to work through the trauma from losing Dad. But it never stuck.

I think she went maybe three times before she gave up and crawled back into bed. Some days are better than others, but ever since Dad died, I've not seen any light in her eyes. It's like there's nothing there. Just…sadness.

"You hav!en't gone to work." Her voice is quiet, weak. I wonder when was the last time she ate something.

"No."

She clears her throat.

"Did you lose your jobs, Janie?"

"River." I sigh. "It's River, Mom. And no. I didn't lose my jobs."

"Ah, yes. Janie is in New York." She swallows, and I can hear the rough sound of it. "Living her best life, not a care in the world for her mother, rotting away in this godforsaken town that took your father."

Mom and Dad never had favorites between us. We were always loved and doted on equally, but after the accident, Mom turned all that love into scorn. No matter how much one of us tried to help, it was never enough. If we weren't both here, suffering the same as her, we were selfish and stupid children.

"Janie has a husband and a full-time job, Mom. She can't just leave and come back here to take care of you."

"Is that what you're doing?" She finally turns her gaze on me, and it breaks my heart all over again. All I want is a mother that loves me, that looks at me like I'm a human being, something precious she created out of love. Not like dirt on the bottom of her shoe.

"Yes. That is what I am doing. I moved back here, and I work two jobs to support both of us."

"You've been in bed for three days. How is that supporting me?"

"Mom."

I sit up and scoot back against the headboard. It's the same twin bed I've had since I was a kid. I'm pretty sure it's the same mattress, too. I don't remember her ever getting either of us a new one. And judging by the lumps, it's definitely old.

"I don't need your lectures," she says, venom dripping from her tone. "I need you to get off your lazy ass and make us some money!"

Red splotches appear on her cheeks, and just that small amount of effort sends her breath heaving. She's so small and weak, and I wonder how much time we actually have left with her.

"I have been working nonstop since I moved back." I swallow thickly. I don't want to cry. I've wasted so many tears on her, and I know she doesn't deserve them anymore. But she's still my mom. I still want her to just *love* me. "We are fine. I'm just not feeling well."

"Not feeling well." She scoffs. "You think I don't hear the rumors around town?"

Not sure how she would. She rarely leaves this house, and when she does, most people avoid her like the plague, not knowing when she'll decide to go off on them or break down. People learned quickly that she was unfortunately beyond help.

"What are you talking about?" I ask, groaning.

"Sleeping with that Black boy."

She side-eyes me, looking at me like I'm some sort of slut for having a relationship. Although, she never did like that family. Once they started taking me in most nights, she thought they were insinuating she couldn't take care of me. She felt the same way about Janie's friends, hating their parents for giving her the love she deserved.

"That's really none of your business."

"While you're staying under my roof, it is!" she all but screams. "I won't have my child being talked about by everyone in town! They're saying he carried you out of a restaurant! In broad daylight! Like he was staking some sort of disgusting claim on you."

This is the most I've heard her speak since I came home.

"Always running around with that family of heathens." She spits the words out with so much disdain it makes me flinch.

"They are not heathens. They are good people."

"Good people." She laughs. "They took my daughter from me, acting like I couldn't take care of you."

"You couldn't!" I finally shout at her. Her empty brown eyes turn on me. "You couldn't take care of me! Or Janie! Dad died, and you may as well have, too. You stopped showing up, stopped making sure there was food in the house or clothes on our backs. And that family took me in and treated me like their own!"

"You were *absent*." My words are practically growls because I will not put up with her talking about Katherine and Clyde like they're horrible people for having big hearts. "They were there when I needed someone to put food in my belly. They gave me a safe, warm place to shower and sleep. And where were you?"

She just stares at me, unimpressed and apathetic.

"I was grieving for your father. I was grieving for the man you and Janie killed."

"Excuse me?" My heart plummets, and my skin goes hot and cold. I've always thought she blamed us, but she's never said it out loud. She's never been *that* cruel. "What did you just say to me?"

"You little brats killed him. He wouldn't have had to take that job if it weren't for you two sucking up all our money."

I take a deep breath and then crawl past her out of my bed. Grabbing my larger suitcase from the closet, I start throwing as many clothes and toiletries in it as I can. Tears are falling, and my heart is shattering. I think I'm going to be sick.

"And just what do you think you're doing?" Her voice is shrill. "You can't leave me! I need you!"

I pause for a moment, take another centering breath, and turn to face her.

"You don't need me, Mother. You need my money, which I will not withhold from you." I run my hands through my hair and laugh sadly at the ceiling. "Not that you deserve it. But unlike you, I'm not going to let my own family starve. I will continue to help you with your bills and supplement what you're getting from Dad's social security.

"But I'm not going to stay here and be your crutch. I'm not going to let you speak to me the way you are or speak about people I love like that." I finish throwing shit in my suitcase and zip it up before turning to look at her again. "You know, Janie and I needed you. You may have lost a husband, but we lost our parents. When Dad died, you left us. Maybe not physically, but you did mentally and emotionally. You willingly left us to fend for ourselves."

"Leave, then." She shrugs and just *looks* at me.

"This isn't what it's supposed to be like, you know. You aren't supposed to hate your children. Your children shouldn't have to beg you for love." My tears finally fall fast and free, and I hiccough on a cry. "You're supposed to love us no matter what."

"I can't love something that took the love of my life away," she says, her voice void of any emotion.

"Mom." I say her name like I'm begging. I'm begging her for something, anything. Any type of love or emotion. I just want her to fucking care about me for once. Her eyes slide to my face.

"I can't even look at you without seeing him," she says, her lip curling in disgust. "Those blue eyes are his, and every time I look at you, I see him. And I hate you for it."

I roll my lips and bite down hard, begging my eyes to stop crying and my heart to stop breaking. I don't know how much more it can take before it just can't hold me upright anymore.

"Okay." I breathe out. "I'll deposit money in your

account until debts are paid off. After that, we're done. And outside of money, I want nothing to do with you. I'll be back to get the rest of my stuff tomorrow. I'd appreciate it if you made yourself scarce."

She doesn't say anything, and I take that as my cue to leave. I wish I could say there was some sort of emotional pull to this house, like happy memories of laughter and love. But there isn't. I can't even see my dad in this house anymore, so there's no point in staying where I'm not wanted. Pulling my suitcase behind me, I walk out of my childhood home and toss my life into my Jeep.

CHAPTER THIRTY-FIVE

Hayes

"WHAT IN THE hell are you doin' out here, boy?"

Pops' voice spooks the horse, and it takes off, causing my foot to slip from the stirrup. I fall straight on my ass as the horse takes off to the other side of the corral. His nostrils flare, and he snorts back at me like I'm the one who caused him the anxiety.

"Tryin' to break that horse," I tell him as I stand up and walk over to where Rhett and Pops are leaning against the fence.

"I can see that," he says. "Not doin' a great job, are ya?"

"Can sense his heartache." Rhett smirks at me.

"Not heartbroken," I tell him. "Nothin' to be heartbroken about."

"Did you or did you not break up with River a few days ago?" Rhett asks.

"Did not." I turn my baseball cap around backward. "Did not break up with her. Just told her I needed some time to think things through."

"Heard she was pretty upset," Pops says, eyeing me like he's close to whacking me upside the head.

"She was," Rhett answers for me. "Poppy all but carried her back to the barn, and I had to follow them into town so Poppy could drive River's Jeep. She was in no state to be drivin' home."

"Which leads me to believe," Pops adds, "that you broke her damn heart."

"Yeah, well. I have a bone to pick with both of you anyway. So I'm glad you're here."

"If this is about that funeral nonsense, save it." Pops gives me one of those stern looks I used to get as a kid. The one that tells you he means some serious business.

"Y'all hid it from me. Both of you, Wells, Momma… I was the one kept out of the loop."

"There was no loop to be in," Rhett tells me. "She came, she said what she needed to say, and she went back to the city to finish her degree."

"She didn't say what she needed to say to me," I correct him.

"She did. You just don't remember it because you were too busy gettin' so drunk you couldn't even form memories." Pops rarely gets angry, and he's never been the type to go off on you when he was mad. He's usually silent, letting you come to the conclusion yourself. But now it seems he's decided to break his silence.

"You were in rough fuckin' shape," Rhett agrees.

"I sat up with you all night, making sure you weren't going to choke on your own vomit. She hung around for a second, kissin' your forehead and whispering to you while you slept. I could see the hurt and the love she had for you, Hayes. But stickin' around to be your crutch was not her job. Lord knows she's had enough of that role when it comes to her momma."

"I didn't expect her to be my crutch, Pops." I sigh and lean forward onto the fence, dropping my head as I try to sort out all the thoughts I've been left alone with for the past few days. "But I sure as hell expected her to stay around and let me know she showed up."

"Why?" Rhett asks. "So you could beg her to stay? Use your grief to sway her thinking?"

"That is not—"

"That may not be what you intended to do," he continues, cutting me off. "But that's sure as hell how she would've felt."

"You think it would've been fair to her for you to use her as a shoulder to cry on after losing your sister?" Pops asks. "She's a good woman, a great woman, actually, and she would've stuck around to be there for you when you needed her. Even though it would've meant forgiving you when you had no right to the forgiveness."

"I lost my sister!" I practically yell at them. "I think that constitutes a 'let bygones be bygones' situation."

"You told me that you understood why she didn't come," Rhett says. "You said that you were an ass, made her feel like shit, and that you understood why she didn't want to be around you."

"Yeah. You're right. I did." I take a deep breath and try to get a handle on my emotions. These past few days have been maddening. My brain is trying to sort through so many conflicting thoughts that I haven't had a moment's peace.

"Before I knew she was here and that she hid it from me, I was able to accept it. Have some sort of peace with the fact that I pushed her away so hard she couldn't even come say goodbye to Addie. I was able to take that fault and live with it."

"So, why is this so different, son?"

"Because she saw me." I look up at Pops with watery eyes. "She saw how fucked I was, and she was able to walk away from that. Doesn't that mean something?"

"Oh, Hayes." He sighs and puts his hand on top of mine, squeezing hard. "What do you think that means? That she doesn't love you?"

I can't even talk right now because if I do, I'm going to start blubbering like a fool. I nod and break eye contact, lookin' down at my boots.

"I think it means she was afraid of how much she

loved you," Rhett tells me, his voice a bit softer than normal. It's lacking its normal grumpy, asshole vibe. "We could all see it. You were the idiot that couldn't. And when she showed up and went to fetch you from that bar... Shit, Hayes. She came back with you lookin' like she was going to keel over with how much worry she was carryin'."

"She loved you then, and she loves you now. Take it from an old fart like me." Pops grins at me. "She loves you, son. That girl has a heart ten times the size of Montana in her chest, and I think she may have been afraid you'd break it all over again had she stayed."

"And the reason she kept it from me?" I ask them. "The reason all y'all kept it from me?"

"Stubborn ass," Pops says, laughing. "As far as the family goes, I can't speak for everyone. But it seems like we all had the same idea...save you the heartache that would come from knowing she was here and left you. At first, I didn't think you'd be able to handle that kind of heartache. You were already so far gone because of Addie."

"You were worse off than I was there for a while." Rhett gives me a sad smile. "We were all worried about you."

"And then time went on, life moved on. You moved, dated, and lived your life. At some point, we just all kind of assumed it didn't matter at that point." Pops gives my hand another squeeze. "We didn't know you were carryin' a torch for her all those years."

He winks at me, and I can't help but laugh.

"I was always carryin' her with me," I tell them both. "Just took me a while to admit it, I guess."

"Or realize she felt the same." Rhett rolls his eyes. "She was so head over heels for you in high school I thought she would trip every time she took a step. Followed you around like a goddamn puppy."

"So," Pops says, steering the conversation back on track. "What are you going to do?"

"Fuck if I know."

"That's not the answer I want to hear," he says, giving me another *are you kidding me* look. "Time to man up, son. You built that big-ass house, kept her in your heart the entire time. You grew up, got your shit together. Now it's time to show the hell up for her."

"You saw her." I nod to Rhett. "How do I come back from that?"

"I'm not touchin' that with a ten-foot pole," he says, holding his hands up. "You gotta figure that shit out on your own. Your woman, your circus."

"I think you both have a lot of talkin' to do," Pops says. "Relationships can't survive if you don't communicate. You think your momma and I survived this long just because the sex is good?"

"Oh, come on!" I groan as Rhett grimaces.

"No, thank you," Rhett says. "Do not need to hear. Did not want to hear."

"Oh, grow up." Pops laughs. "How do you think all five of you came about, huh?"

"Jesus Christ." Rhett and I are both unwell in this moment.

"Had to keep tryin' for a girl." Pops smirks at both of us. "Your momma wouldn't let us quit."

"Okay, thank you. Thank you for that," I tell him, hoping he'll shut up now. "I'll figure it out, okay? I'll fix it."

"Hell, is that all I had to do? Gross you out?" Pops laughs again. "Should've tried that sooner." His eyes slide to Rhett. "Should've tried it with you."

"And I'm out." Rhett throws his hand up in a wave and starts backing away.

"Fix it, son," Pops says, pointing at me as he starts to follow Rhett. "And give that horse a break. You have no fuckin' clue what you're doin' when it comes to breaking horses."

"Or when it comes to women," I hear Rhett mumble.

"Hah! Good one." Pops slaps him on the back.

"Glad I could entertain y'all for a bit!" I call out to them.

Pops just waves.

Now to figure out how in the hell to fix this shit.

CHAPTER THIRTY-SIX

River

I SLEPT IN MY JEEP, and let me tell you, it was not comfortable. There wasn't enough room to lay down the back seats and make a type of bed, so I just had to recline the seat and hope for the best. I didn't know where to park it so I wouldn't be disturbed, so I just drove out to the nearest campsite and hoped I'd be left alone.

But now I *have* to go back to work tomorrow. I can't afford to miss any more days, and I have to shower. I was too depressed and wallowing in my own misery for the past three days that I haven't brushed my hair, let alone taken a whole-ass shower.

I could go to one of our motels, but truthfully, they're not in the best shape, and it's not like I have a ton of money to throw around. Especially not now when

I'm going to have to find a place to rent ASAP. I need to save all the money I can.

There's no other family in town, and I can't show up at Evie's. One, I have no idea where she lives. And two, I don't think we're close enough for that. The only other people I'm close enough to in this town are the Blacks. But showing up at Katherine and Clyde's door is not on my to-do list.

So, instead, I call Poppy.

"Hey! How are you? Are you taking care of yourself?" The first words out of her mouth make my tear ducts act up again.

"Hey." I clear my throat and try to stop the tears. "So, I kind of can't go back to my mom's house, and I was wondering if maybe I could stay with you in the cabin until I can get a place to stay?"

"Of course." Her answer comes quickly. "I'm basically living with Rhett anyway, so just head on over, and I'll meet you there. You can have the whole dang thing."

"No, Poppy, I—"

"Meet you there."

She hangs up, and my heart squeezes. She fits right in with that family, kind and caring. I'm thankful to have met her this summer. And I know that when I show up on her doorstep, she isn't going to judge me for the rat's nest on top of my head or for the fact that I'm in wrinkled old clothes with a spaghetti stain on the front. She'll just accept me and support me.

The drive to the ranch only takes about twenty minutes, and when I pull into the little driveway that leads to the cabin she was staying in, I see her sitting on the front porch, swinging her feet off the railing. She jumps down when I pull in and runs to the driver's side of my car. When I step out, she throws her arms around me and holds me tight.

"Rhett gave me some spare sheets, so I ran over here and changed the bed. I've got everything I need over at his place, so you take your time. Hell, move in if you want." Her smile is wide as she looks me over. "Not like any of them are going to care."

"You told Rhett not to tell Hayes, right?" I'm already looking around, wondering if he's going to jump out from behind a tree.

"He has promised not to tell." She mimes zipping her lips and throwing away the key. "But I will say, while this little place is tucked away, it won't stop him from seeing your Jeep here if he happens to mosey over this way."

"Good point." I look around. "I'll pull in behind the house. Might give me some time before he catches me."

"Okay, that works." She laughs. "Now, can I help you carry stuff in?"

"I only have the one suitcase. I told Mom I'd come back for the rest of my stuff today." I bite my lip and look at her. "Maybe you could come with? I'm dreading the trip, honestly."

"At your service! Rhett told Wells that I wasn't feeling well, so you have me all day."

"Thank you, Poppy." I pull her back in for another hug.

"Of course." She smiles and shrugs. "What are friends for?"

After a hot shower, a lot of conditioner, and a very awkward trip into my mom's, my stomach has stopped its incessant anxious burning. I'm feeling lighter and happier. Knowing I don't have to go back there and soak up all that sadness has lifted a lot of weight off my shoulders.

It's getting cooler outside, the autumn weather starting to trickle in at night. But we have the windows open as we sip on a glass of wine and let *Sex and the City* play in the background.

"Isn't it crazy?" she asks, drawing my attention away from the sunset outside and back to her. "How much the fresh air can just chill you out?"

"Mhm," I hum, smiling over at her. "It's always helped me with that. It's kind of magical here. No matter how bad things got at home, I knew I could always come here and feel a little bit at peace."

"I'm sorry you went through that, River." She bridges the gap between us and squeezes my forearm. "Back then and this morning. I can't even begin to imagine how hard it's been."

"Her outburst today kind of gave me clarity," I

confess. "Just because they're a parent doesn't mean they're a *good* parent. And I deserve a lot better than what she has given me since Dad died. I'm sure I'll have my moments where I miss her, and I'm sure it won't be easy to go no contact, but it's what I need for my own mental health."

"What about the money?" she asks. "Not that you have to tell me. It is none of my business."

"No, it's okay. I don't mind." I sit my glass down on the side table behind me. "I told her I would still deposit money into her account. And I will. Until the creditors are off her back, I'll dig her out of the hole. But once the amount is paid, I'm washing my hands fully of her. If Janie wants to take care of her from there, she can. But I'm out."

"And…Hayes?" Her voice goes quiet. "I am almost afraid to ask. Have you heard from him at all?"

"No." I scoff. "This is why I hate the term 'space.' What does it mean? When's the cutoff? Does giving him space allow him to go be with someone else? Does it mean we don't talk at all?" I groan and drop my head back.

"I think it means something different for everyone." Poppy sighs. "And that's what makes it so goddamn hard."

Her phone buzzes. Again. It's been going off for the past hour, and I know I've hogged her for long enough.

"You can go, Poppy," I tell her. "Seriously. I didn't

get any sleep last night, and I have two shifts to work tomorrow."

"Are you sure?" Her eyebrows pinch together. "I feel bad. I wanted to stay here until I tucked you in and you were passed out cold. No alone time for your mind to go all dark and scary."

That makes me laugh.

"I promise you that I am okay. Some alone time would probably be nice."

"If you insist." She stands and clears the wine, corking the bottle and putting it in the fridge. "But if you need anything, just text me. I will happily sleep on the couch and come give you all the cuddles."

"I think Rhett would literally kill me if I stole you from his bed."

"Please." She rolls her eyes. "That man needs to learn how to miss me anyway."

"Hey." I take her arm as she walks out the front door. "Thank you. Seriously. I don't know what I would've done without you today."

"Oh, River." She pulls me into a bone-crushing hug.

"Go, go." I sniff and wipe the lone little tear that tries to escape. "Go get laid."

She gives me a playful shove and then skips down the stairs, leaving me alone with the crickets and my thoughts. I turn off the outdoor light and close all the windows and curtains. It needs to look like no one is here. All the lights are out except for one small one next to the bed, and I leave it on. It's not that I'm afraid of the dark or of being alone out here, but there's something about leaving it on that gives me some comfort.

I feel like if I turn it off, the silence will be too loud. Or my thoughts will be. And right now, all I want is a really, really good night's sleep. Scooting down under the covers, I breathe in the scent of laundry detergent and fabric softener.

My phone vibrates.

Poppy: Melatonin is in the nightstand. Use it. And set a loud alarm!

Me: I think I love you.

I dig out the melatonin and dry swallow one pill. Making sure my alarm is set and my volume is on loud, I flip my phone over and pull the covers up to my chin. Within fifteen minutes, the exhaustion wins, and I'm out cold.

CHAPTER THIRTY-SEVEN

River

I GOT the best night's sleep of my life last night. I know I was exhausted, but I think the melatonin helped me stay asleep. Pretty sure I woke up in the same position I fell asleep in. Poppy told me to help myself to the groceries, even though there aren't many since she's basically moved in with Rhett. But there's coffee, and that's all a girl can ask for.

Plugging my phone in to charge, I scroll through my playlists and find the best one for lifting my spirits. Sometimes there are just certain songs that make you want to dance your heart out while you throw your head back and sing with your whole chest. That's the playlist I put on, and as I get ready for my day, the music infects my mood and raises my spirits.

I dance around the small house, swinging from room to room as I drink my coffee and throw on some clothes.

This is the first time since everything happened with Hayes that I've had any energy to move around, let alone stretch my muscles and *smile*. It feels good and makes me think I can finally have a day without crying my eyes out.

I'm just finishing up when I hear a gentle knock at the door. Nervous butterflies take flight in my stomach because I am fully expecting it to be Hayes. But when I walk out of the bedroom, I see Katherine standing at the door, waving at me with one hand while the other holds a huge plate of breakfast. My god, this woman. No wonder Clyde locked her down.

"Hi!" I open the door and gesture for her to come in. "You brought me breakfast?"

"Of course!" She walks in and sits it down on the island in the kitchen. "Rhett told me last night you would be staying here, and I knew with Poppy mostly living with Rhett now, there'd be hardly any food in this place."

"Thank you so much." My stomach growls as I pull up a chair, too hungry to act otherwise. "This looks so good."

"Care if I sit with you? I know you probably have work today…"

"Please." I push out a chair with my foot. "I don't have to leave for another fifteen minutes or so."

"How are you?" Her face goes soft, and I can see all

the love she has for me there. Like a mother should have. "Something happen with your mom?"

"I'm just tired of taking care of her when she never took care of me. And on top of that, I don't even get any love in return for taking care of her. This fight we had was kind of the last straw."

"I'm so sorry, River." She leans forward and gives me a hug.

"I'm sorry for crashing. I just need a place to stay until I can get on my feet. I've been saving up for my own place with the tips I get from the bar and—"

"River." She lays her hand on top of mine. "You could live in this cabin your entire life if you wanted. Or any of the little houses we have dotted around for the workers. We don't care. You're our daughter, and we want to take care of you just like we do the other kids."

"Thank you." I have to whisper the words because she has my emotions running haywire.

"Just stay here until everything with your mom's stuff is settled. Or if Poppy wants to keep this one in case she gets sick of Rhett, take a different one." She smirks over at me. "Maybe one that is on the other side of the property, as far away from Hayes as you can get."

I laugh.

"Did you see I tried to hide my car?" I nod in the direction of where I hid it. "Was hoping I could get in and out without him noticing."

"Not sure how long that'll last," she says, picking a

piece of hash brown off my plate. "But I won't say a word. You deserve a little bit of peace."

"Can I ask how he's doing?"

"He's okay." She sighs and leans forward on her elbows. "I guess Rhett and Clyde had a little chat with him the other day, tryin' to set him straight. But you know Hayes. He's always been stubborn as a mule."

"He has." I give her a weak laugh. "But I kind of really fucked up this time."

"And he didn't?" She raises an eyebrow. "The way I see it, you both did some things you aren't too happy about. He hurt you, you hurt him. But it's time to look past that and see the love you have for one another. End of the day, that's what matters."

"He said he needed space." I cringe. "I hate that word. I never know what it means."

"He'll come around." She hops off the barstool and kisses my cheek. "Try to stick it out a little while longer. If it's meant to happen, it will. If not…" She shrugs. "Then you're still my daughter, and I still love you."

"Thank you, Katherine." My eyes are watering as I smile at her.

"Let me know what you and Poppy want to do about living arrangements," she tells me as she walks toward the door. "If she wants to keep this one for herself, we'll get another one cleaned up for you."

"Tell Clyde I said hi."

"I will, dear. Have a good day at work. And let me know if my son gives you any more trouble."

She winks as she slips out the door, and her lightness makes me laugh. Getting to talk to both her and Poppy has lifted my spirits a bit. I have a place to stay, I'm still employed, and I still have friends and family. Things could be so much worse.

But that doesn't stop me from peeking through the blinds on every side of the house after I'm done eating, making sure the coast is clear before I walk out to my Jeep. It's not that I think I can avoid him forever, especially living on the same property as him. Part of me even kind of *wants* to run into him. But I need to rehearse what I'm going to say first or something because I do not want to walk into that situation without being able to hold my own.

Leaving a few minutes early, I drive over to the rescue barn, making sure I don't see Hayes before I jump out and run in to say good morning to Betty. Poppy and Wells are already there, letting the dogs out to stretch their legs before their breakfast. Betty is in the center of the barn, lying on her back as a puppy chews on one of her paws.

When she sees me, she jumps up to her feet and comes running over to me. We've made so much progress it warms my freaking heart.

"My sweet girl, mistreated and misunderstood," I

murmur as I leave a trail of kisses down her nose. "We've come so far, haven't we?"

"Should take her to the cabin after you get off tonight," Wells says, smiling at us. "She's ready, and it would give you some company out there."

"That's a great idea!" Poppy is all smiles. "I'll get all of her stuff together for you and leave it next to her room so you can just grab her and go after your shift at the bar."

"Does Hayes know?" I ask, looking at Wells.

"Wouldn't surprise me if he can just sense it." He shrugs, a smirk playing on his mouth. "He can scent you like a damn bloodhound."

"Gross." Poppy's nose scrunches up.

"Yeah, I agree. That's gross. Please don't talk about my scent being so strong a man can literally *scent* me. Like I'm something to be hunted down."

"I dunno," he says, his face looking ornery as hell. "I think the hunt is all part of the fun."

"I'm not going to kink shame you, Wells Black." I laugh with him because I think back to Hayes chasing after me to the stream. And Wells is right, that shit is pretty damn fun. "But please refrain from telling me about the dirty deeds you do in the woods."

"Just don't be lookin' out your windows at night." He winks at me. "And you won't have to worry about seeing a thing."

"Well, now I'm intrigued," Poppy says. "Maybe this is something I need to explore with Rhett."

"Maybe coordinate," I joke. "That way, y'all both aren't running around naked outside at the same time. Would hate to latch onto the wrong partner."

Poppy lets out a loud laugh at that.

"Can you *imagine* what Rhett would do!" She laughs even harder. "Shit. It would be worth it just to see his face."

"No, thank you," Wells counters. "I am quite attached to my balls, and that man would rip them off without a second thought."

"That I believe." I give Betty one more kiss. "I've gotta get going. I'll pick her up tonight after my shift. Oh, and Poppy? Katherine stopped by this morning and chatted about living arrangements. Can I call you later?"

"Sure thing." She smiles, and her cheeks blush. "Maybe not during my lunch break, though…"

"Gross. You guys are too happy," I tease her and roll my eyes. "Keep that shit to yourselves."

She sticks her tongue out at me.

"Have a good day!" they both call out as I leave.

"Thanks, guys!"

I walk back to my car, and my cheeks hurt from smiling so much. God, my heart is so much lighter than it was just twenty-four hours ago. It's crazy what getting out of an unhappy home will do for your mental health.

Shoving my key into the ignition, my Jeep turns over, and when I look up to buckle my seat belt, Hayes is standing on the front porch of his momma's house, staring right at me.

Good mood gone.

Not sure what to do, I raise my hand in a small wave. He does the same and starts to walk down the stairs.

No, no, no. Not yet. Not right now.

I throw the gear shift into reverse and damn near spin out as I try to escape him. His face is unreadable in my rearview, and I can't help glancing back at him until he's out of sight.

I take a deep breath. This is going to be harder than I thought.

CHAPTER THIRTY-EIGHT

Hayes

WELL, that wasn't how I wanted that to go. I figured the first time I saw River would be more orchestrated and I'd have time to ease her into talking to me. But the way she looked at me just now as she practically did dough-nuts getting down our drive, I don't think she's ready yet.

I check my watch. It's early for her to be visiting Betty, but when she's staying on the property, I guess it's easier for her to make time. She's probably hoping I don't know she's here, but Pops is horrible at keeping secrets. He came over yesterday when Momma told him she was moving in for the foreseeable future.

Pops gave me another good talkin'-to, making sure I knew I wasn't to bother her. I'm supposed to stay out of her way until she's ready to come to me. But that makes all of zero sense to me since I'm the one that asked for space. It has to be me that goes to her. End this stupid shit.

Because, yeah. I'm tired of finding things to get angry about. I'm tired of spending time and energy on things that aren't love for River. And I do love her. So now I just need to tell her and try to put all of this nonsense behind us. I'm ready to start fresh for real this time and give her all the things she deserves.

"She's quicker than a cat on a hot tin roof," Pops says, walking up behind me. "Never seen someone peel out of this driveway that fast."

"Haulin' ass." I grin over at him.

"Think you can help your brother get the cattle ready for the fair this week? I know a lot of the guys have their own shit goin' on with the festivities and their own kids. He could use the extra hand."

The fair is a weeklong event starting on Monday, which means we've got to get our shit together today and then haul cattle over there tomorrow. They open the gates a day early, letting everyone come in and set up. It takes a few days, but the main shows and activities don't start 'til later in the week anyway. A lot of ranchers actually end up stayin' there if they're out of town, parking RV's and shit on-site. Luckily, we live close enough where we can lock up the animals and come home for the night.

"Yeah, I figured I needed to head out and find him. Gonna stop in and see Poppy, then I'll head out."

"Don't bother her either," Pops says, givin' me a stern look.

"Not gonna bother her." I roll my eyes and walk the rest of the way down the steps. "Just gonna say hi to my sister-in-law."

Dad's eyes go a little soft and misty as he looks out over the ranch. Of course, Poppy isn't actually my sister-in-law yet. But she may as well be because there ain't no way Rhett is going to let that one go. And I like thinking I have a sister again.

"Nice to have another daughter to dote on," Pops tells me, his voice quiet. "And I'd like another. So, maybe hurry your ass up with River."

"I'm trying. But someone told me to steer clear."

"Since when do you listen to your old man?" he calls out after me.

"Good point!"

He laughs and goes back inside, probably ready to sit back in his recliner for the rest of the morning watching Westerns. That man has probably seen every episode of *Gunsmoke* twenty times by now. It's just on repeat, and I don't know how Momma stands it.

I make my way over to the rescue barn, and both Wells and Poppy greet me but won't look at me. They're very good at pretending to be so busy they can't even look in my direction. Lord, no one in this family has a poker face besides Momma.

"Y'all can stop ignoring me," I tell them. "I know

she's staying in the cabin, and I know I'm supposed to be a good boy and leave her be."

"You? Be a good boy?" Wells asks. "That's laughable."

"How do you know?" Poppy ignores Wells as she stops what she's doing and puts her hands on her hips.

"You think anyone in this family can keep a secret?"

She groans and drops her head back as she throws her hands up in surrender.

"I'm not going to tell you to leave her alone," Poppy says, surprising me. "Because I think both of you need to get over yourselves and hash it out."

"Fuck it out, more like," Wells murmurs.

"Wells Black." Poppy gives him a look.

"Just sayin'." He shrugs and gives her one of his cheeky grins.

"She's coming back tonight after her shift at the bar to pick up Betty and her things. She decided to take her to the cabin."

I reach into my back pocket, fingering the small note I wrote this morning. I planned on going over to the cabin and tucking it into the screen door or something, but maybe I can just hide it in Betty's things instead.

"Can I leave the note I wrote for her? Like with Betty's stuff?"

Poppy smiles and nods, holding out her hand.

I hesitate.

"I'm not going to read it," she says with a sigh. "I

promise. I just don't have her stuff put together yet. I promise you I will guard it with my life and make sure she gets it."

"Not for his eyes," I tell her as I place it in her palm. "And I'll know if he does because he'll never let me live it down."

"I swear." She smiles at me. "I may be short, but it just helps my agility. I could take him if I needed to."

"I'm not touching you," Wells jokes. "Like I said, I'm attached to my balls."

Not knowing what *that* means, nor wanting to know, I leave my note with Poppy and the ball in River's court.

CHAPTER THIRTY-NINE

River

"HEY THERE, BUG!" Bill greets me as I walk into the bar. It's a Saturday night, so I'm already dreading the crowd that will come with it later.

"Hey, Bill!" The soles of my shoes stick to the floor as I walk over to the bar. Not because it's dirty, per se. We do mop. I think there's just been so much whiskey spilled in this place over the last fifty years it's become part of the woodwork. "Thanks again for giving me some time off this week."

"I keep tellin' you to take time off. It was about time you started listenin'." He looks at me out of the corners of his eyes while he works on drying all the pint glasses. "Everything alright?"

"Sure." I laugh and shrug. "As good as it can be, I guess. How were things this week without me?"

Walking to the room that's just behind the bar, I toss

my bag down at the desk and clock in. Bill's old-school, making all of us write down our times on a paper log, which he then adds up…with a calculator. And not the one that comes on his phone. No, no. He whacks out one of the ones my grandma used to use when she tallied up her checkbook. It has a little paper scroll at the top and makes very loud noises when you hit the Enter button.

"Pretty good, actually. That Hayes kid had a good turnout on Thursday."

Shit. I totally forgot about Hayes playing every Thursday. A little pit of guilt forms in my stomach for not being here to support him.

"Mostly women, mind you," he says with a laugh, probably because I left out the little detail about how Hayes and I were kind of dating. "But still, good crowd. You can tell him I'll start putting him on the schedule for some weekends. Think he'd like that?"

"I'm sure he would." I try to smile, but I know it falls flat. I didn't like the girls throwing themselves at Hayes when I was here and could stake my claim. But it feels even worse to know they were doing it when we were taking space and I was wallowing in my own self-pity.

"I tried to grab him to let him know before he left, but that boy had a fire under his ass." He chuckles. "Jumped off the stage and dodged everyone in sight. Must've had something to get to. Anyway, let him know just to pop in or give me a call. We'll set up some new times for him."

"He'll love that." It becomes a little easier to smile now knowing that Hayes dipped out. Maybe he was trying to outrun Ashley and her cronies. "I'll let him know next time I see him."

Bill lets the conversation drop after that, and I spend the rest of the afternoon cleaning and getting ready to open. And the night goes by pretty quickly. Too soon, Rhett and Poppy, Hayes, and Wells all walk in. I want to shrivel up and blow away. It's just me and one other person besides Bill tending the bar, and I have a feeling those boys are going to seek me out.

My palms are sweating as I watch them all look around, finding an open table, and then my stomach roars up into my throat when Hayes looks at the bar and finds me with shocking accuracy. But a small smile is all I get, and then he's walking off with Wells to grab their table.

"Hi, pretty lady!" Poppy shouts across the bar. Her smile is infectious. Even Rhett is grinning as he watches her stand on her tiptoes to reach across and kiss my cheeks. "We told Hayes to leave you alone since you're at work."

"I didn't tell Hayes shit," Rhett grumbles. "I don't get involved."

"Yes, yes." Poppy rolls her eyes. "*I* told Hayes to leave you alone. Rhett is grumpy and doesn't like to participate. But while you're working is not the time. So I sent him to the table with Wells."

"Thank you." I smile and try my hardest not to search him out. This might be a long night. "What can I get you?"

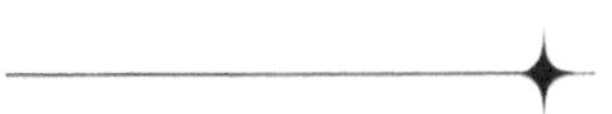

Hayes actually kept his word to Poppy and stayed away for the entire night. It was like old times, before we were friends again and he and I weren't talking. He just sat there, sipping on that single drink and giving half-assed chat to his brothers. Our eyes met a few times throughout the night, and each time, it felt like I was being pulled over to him. I just wanted to forget about our space and run to him.

But I just don't know where his head is at yet.

I pull into the driveway and try to slowly pull in front of the rescue barn. It only takes me a few minutes to gather up all of Betty's things and then get her in the car. I think this is the first time riding in a car since she got here, but she does so well. The window is rolled down for her, and she gets all the sniffs on the way over to the cabin.

Once I get her in the house after she's gone potty, it's like she's a completely different dog almost. She sniffs around and then is wagging her tail as she runs from one side of the house to the other. Her zoomies are hilarious, her nails trying to grip on the wood floors as she slips and slides.

"Let's get you set up for sleep," I tell her through my laughter. "We need to get our beauty rest."

As I start to unpack her things, a folded-up piece of notebook paper falls out. It's just plain lined paper, ripped haphazardly, with my name on the front. I immediately recognize Hayes' writing. I run my thumb over the pen strikes as my world kind of stands still for a moment.

When I open this, it's going to say one of two things. He's either telling me good news or bad news. Of course, I hope it's good news, but I'm so scared he's over trying with me that I can't face it right now. Not until I'm settled in bed and have the comfort of a weighted blanket over my body.

So I get Betty set up, laying her bed on the floor next to me with a ton of soft blankets. I tried to get her to jump up on the bed and sleep with me, but she was having none of it. Maybe once she gets more comfortable, she will. And, let's be honest, after spending months in a barn, she isn't the cleanest. The bedsheets are probably better off.

Once she's down and snoring quite loudly, I hold the little note in my hand and flip it over and over between my fingers. I smell it, for some weird reason, but it just smells like paper. Not sure why I thought I'd be able to smell him on it. I take a deep breath and start to unfold it. I do it painfully slowly, annoying myself. But then it's open, and his handwriting is carefully scrawled across the page.

Hey Firefly,

This little note is just that... little. There are so many things I want to say to you, but I don't want to write them down. I want to tell you to your face. But more than that, I want your permission to do so. I know I'm the one that told you I needed space, a moment to breathe, and so I know it's up to <u>me</u> to come to <u>you</u>. And I want to — I will.

But I need you to be okay with that first, because I know I hurt you, and I don't know if you're ready to have this talk.

If you are, just shoot me a text, and I'll come running.

If you aren't, just ignore this, and I'll try again soon.

I'll try again and again until you're ready.

I'm done with the space, River. I don't need space from you. I just need you.

- Hayes

I wipe the few tears that have rolled down my cheeks and take a steadying breath. I love that he didn't throw all of his feelings into a letter. I would prefer to hear him say the things he needs to say. But I do appreciate letting me know he doesn't want this to end. I can finally have some peace knowing that Hayes still wants me. He still wants this.

So I fold the piece of paper back up, lay it on my nightstand, and turn out the light. I unlock my phone, stare at the old text message conversation between the two of us, and let my thumbs hover over the letters. He said he would come running, but I don't want to do this when he's been out and I'm exhausted from a long day. Instead, I lock my phone and shove it under my pillow.

We can wait one more day.

CHAPTER FORTY

River

I LIED TO MYSELF. I was fully committed to texting Hayes the next morning, but then I thought I should get ready first, just in case he actually does run right over. So I showered and got ready for the day, comfy clothes and my hair braided. Because no one wants to be in denim on their day off. And by the time I was done, Katherine was knocking on the door again, bringing me a plate of hot food.

"You have got to stop doing this," I tell her as I open the door and let her in. "You have too many other things to worry about."

"Oh, hush." She pets Betty on the top of the head and then sits the plate down on the island before making coffee. "You're what I'm worrying about right now, so just let me. Gives me something to do."

"Katherine. Oh, my god. This is way too much

food!" I peel back the foil, and the plate is just piled high.

"It's not just for you," she says, laughing as she pulls out a couple of plates. "I figured I'd eat with you this morning. It's gorgeous outside, so we can sit out on the front porch and enjoy it."

A few minutes later and Betty is lying out in the grass, eyes squinting toward the sun as she bakes in it. She's still tied up on a long lead because I don't quite trust her yet not to run off. That's going to take some training. Katherine and I have eaten the amazing food she brought, and we're just enjoying the sounds of the ranch as we sip our coffee.

"You spoken to him yet?" she finally asks.

"No. But I plan to today." I grin and drop my head back on the rocker, closing my eyes. "He left me a little note and told me to tell him when I was ready to talk."

"If you don't hear from him right away, he's helping Rhett and the other boys transport cattle to the fairgrounds. Probably going to be busy all day."

"I totally forgot it's the fair!"

I love the fair. Especially the days before it gets busy on Friday and Saturday. During the week, it's quieter, with only the ranchers and farmers there for animal shows during the day and barn dancing at night. All the food trucks are set up, though, so you get to go through all the delicious food without the long lines. I can already taste the homemade lemonade and deep-fried funnel cake.

"They're gonna be busy bees for the next couple of days, that's for sure. I know Rhett is ready to make some money on those cows." She picks up the empty plates and carries everything back into the kitchen.

"Leave those in the sink!" I call after her. "I will never forgive you if you wash those dishes!"

"Fine, fine!" The old floor creaks as she walks back outside. "I better get goin'. Clyde is watching the babies for me while I'm over here, and god knows what he's lettin' them get into."

"I'll pray for you!" I tell her as she laughs and walks out into the yard. She stops and gives Betty some belly scratches before walking the rest of the way home. I stay out on the porch for a while longer, listening to the sounds and letting Betty wear herself out with watching squirrels she's never going to catch.

Once we're back inside, I pick my phone up to text Hayes. I have so many nervous butterflies that I'm a little worried the food might come back up. Will he even have time to talk today? Should I wait to text him until tomorrow when he'll be less busy?

My thumbs begin typing and then stop, hovering over the keyboard with uncertainty. This should not be this scary. And when the phone vibrates with a text, I almost drop it. Christ, I'm on edge.

Hayes: Saw the typing bubbles pop up while I was checking my phone.

I huff out a laugh.

Me: That's creepy.

Hayes: Can we talk?

Me: Your momma said you're busy today. Fair stuff.

Hayes: I'm never too busy for you, darlin'.

Me: Cheesy.

Hayes: Stop making me chase you through this damn phone. Meet me out here later. I'll treat you to dinner.

Me: Will there be funnel cake?

Hayes: And lemonade…

Me: Fine.

HAYES

"Why're you smilin' like a fool?" Rhett asks as he walks out of the barn. Wells is close behind, wiping his hands on an old rag. We've been getting the cattle transported and settled in for the last six hours, and we're all filthy and fuckin' tired.

I only checked my phone when we were done because I thought maybe she'd had enough time to think about my note. I was hoping for a text. But when I saw the bubbles pop up and disappear, pop up and disappear, I knew she just needed another nudge. So I decided *fuck it* and messaged her instead. Happy to report it worked.

"River finally cave?" Wells asks before I can answer.

"She's coming out this evening." I shift anxiously from foot to foot. This woman kills me, leaves me anxious and excited all at the same time. I know the rest of this afternoon is gonna go by so slowly. "Gonna give her a proper little date and then take her dancin'."

"Well, you smell like shit," Rhett says, clapping me on the shoulder. "Maybe take a shower first."

"Everything settled?" I ask, hoping we can head back now to give me enough time.

"Settled enough." I get one of Rhett's rare smiles as he notices my excitement. "We can head back. I'll finish in the mornin'."

The truck reeks on the way home, the cab filled with three very dirty, very smelly men. We have to roll down the windows because I just can't handle the filth. I practically fall out of the truck when we finally make it back, desperate to get away from the stench.

"Spare Poppy the eye-watering smell of you and throw those clothes out. Honestly, just have her leave the house until you're clean." I hold my nose and wave my hand in front of my face.

I only get an annoyed grunt from Rhett.

"Good luck tonight, man," Wells says, clapping me on the shoulder before tugging me into a hug.

"I'll see you guys tonight," I tell them. "I'll be bringing River to the dance."

"I tried to get out of it," Rhett groans. "But Poppy really wants to go and experience it. So do the kids."

The locals always get together and put on a party in one of the show barns on the first night. It lets everyone come together and chat. There are people from all over the county that come in, bringing their families with them. So we all get to know each other, and it's nice to have a night to hang out and have some fun before all the hard work starts up.

River has always loved the fair. We used to go as kids, running all over the grounds, eating far too much sugar and riding all the rides. We'd sneak into the animal barns so she could look at all the bunnies and pet all the pigs. And while the adults were catching up and line dancing inside, we'd be outside, practicing our own dance moves in the grass. Close enough to hear the music but far enough away that we wouldn't get caught being out too late.

I can't wait to see her and hold her. It's taking all my strength not to run over to the little cabin she's staying in and wrap her in my arms. Right now, though, I'm afraid she'd gag. So I go home instead, washing my body and my hair a few times to make sure the sweat and stink is out. I dress in the Wranglers that always make her stare at my ass and a shirt of mine she liked to wear to bed. I like having a little piece of her with me.

Finishing touch: a backward baseball hat. Because that girl goes nuts for it.

I've been rehearsing all the things I want to say to her in my head for days now. Honestly, since I got home the day of our fight, I've been trying to find the words I want to say. There's so many, and I don't want to ramble on and on. I just want to get my point across. I want her to know that I love her and that I need her in my life. That she's my best friend and the person I want to spend my life with.

It's simple. I love her, and I'm tired of us getting in the way of that.

I text her as I climb into my truck.

> Me: Meet you at the front gates in an hour?

> River: See you there, cowboy.

CHAPTER FORTY-ONE

River

HAYES IS WAITING on me as I pull up to the front gates. No one is there to open them yet, so he does it for me, and I park off to the side where I won't be in anyone's way. The nerves are really churning now, making my hands shake as I turn off the engine. He's back there, locking the gates again while I try to control my breathing.

"You can do this, River." I look at myself in the visor mirror. My hair is straight and down, and I've done my makeup a little. I've even paired my dusty boots with a dress. "Woman up."

He knocks on my window and makes me jump so high I almost whack my head on the roof of the car. Hayes just laughs as I flick the visor back and climb out.

"Good to see you, firefly." He's all happy smiles and

sexy eyes. That backward baseball hat does something to my lady bits, and it's really unfair that he can make something so simple look so good.

"Hi" is all I manage. My mouth seems to have stopped working.

"So, I thought we could have a little dinner. Almost all the trucks are set up, and we can get what you want and then take it to the grandstands."

His eyes are lit up from the inside out. He looks good…damn good.

"Alright, then. Lead the way."

The whole thing is set up in a horseshoe shape about the track, where they do horse races, derbies, and tractor pulls. One side is where all the animals are, and the other has the rides and fun stuff for kids. And as you walk on the paved road that leads you around the whole thing, you get assaulted by food truck after food truck, serving everything from pizza to chicken on a stick to elephant ears and funnel cakes.

When we were really little, Katherine and Clyde would walk us around, letting us choose whatever we wanted. I would always get chicken fried rice and a funnel cake topped with extra powdered sugar. By the time I had downed all of that *and* a lemonade, which I'm sure had a cup of sugar per glass, I was bouncing off the damn walls. It's a good thing we ate first and ran off all the energy.

"Getting the same thing you used to get as a kid, I

see." Hayes smiles at me as he holds my rice and we wait on the funnel cake to come out.

"It's not the fair unless you almost give yourself diabetes."

Once it comes out, piping hot and smelling of sweet, delicious dough, I hold on to it for dear life as we climb the concrete stairs between the bleachers. He's laid a few blankets over the hard metal and even set up a little vase with a few wildflowers and a candle.

This is probably the cutest fucking thing I've ever seen.

"So, I know we're eating, and I know I should probably wait, but I really can't anymore."

My mouth is full of chicken and rice, so I just nod in his direction as I feel my stomach fall through my butt.

"I don't want to fight anymore. I don't want to keep finding things to be mad at each other about. I'm an idiot, and I never should've reacted the way I did. If I could go back to that moment, River, I would change everything about it. Watching you walk away, crying and holding on to Poppy... It was like watching you walk away ten years ago."

"I shouldn't have hid it from you. I'm sorry." I sigh and look down at my plate, feeling a little ashamed of myself. "I kept wanting to tell you, but I was honestly just so afraid. Afraid of you leaving or afraid that you'd be upset I came home at all..."

"I should've listened to you." He reaches across the

little gap between us and takes my hand. His skin is tanned a warm brown from all the hours working in the sun, and I love the way his calluses rub against my knuckles.

"I hate how I reacted, River. I let my ego get in the way, and I'm sorry. I'm sorry for asking for space and pushing you away like that. I'm sorry that I was one more person in your life that you felt you couldn't rely on. I'm sorry I wasn't there for you when the fight happened with your mom."

I raise an eyebrow, wondering how he heard about that one.

"You think Momma could keep that to herself?" He smirks. "She spilled the beans so fast. And it made me hate myself. I should've been there for you. You should've felt like you could come to me instead of living on your own in that little cabin. I should've never asked for space, Riv. I should've held you through it instead of pushing you away."

"You deserved that space, though, Hayes." I look him in the eyes and squeeze his hand as I try to convey how much I understand him needing that. "Maybe we both needed it. Life needed to give us one more test before letting us be together." I try to laugh, but it comes out a little pathetic. "If you still want to be together like that…"

He tugs on the hand that he's holding, almost making me knock over the food in front of us. I stand at the last moment, avoiding disaster, before he pulls me down to his lap. And I sink into him, wrapping my arms around his neck and breathing him in. He holds me tight, his hands rubbing up and down my back as we just hold each other.

"I want you, River. Only you, forever you." He hugs me tighter and kisses my shoulder and my hair before tugging my face back so he can look at me, his blue eyes searching mine. "And I want everything with you. Anything and everything you want out of this life, I want that, too. I want to come home every day with you sittin' barefoot on the front porch waiting for me. I want to wake up every morning and see your pretty face. I want late-night swims and Sunday cobblers.

"My best friend," he continues, pushing my hair out of my face as he looks at me with nothing but adoration. "I love you. I am so fuckin' in love with you, firefly."

The tears start falling now, and I can't stop them. But for the first time in a long time, they're happy tears. I let them fall and lean forward, grabbing his mouth with mine. I kiss and kiss and kiss him. I've missed the way he tastes and how soft his lips are.

"I love you, too," I whisper against his mouth before I kiss him again. We get lost in each other, completely ignoring our surroundings and the food I was previously so excited for. It's just me and Hayes, holding on as we find each other all over again.

And I've gotta say, teenage River would be fucking stoked right now.

"No more runnin'," he murmurs against my lips. "From either one of us, yeah?"

"Promise."

His hands move to my hips, and the kiss turns into something more very quickly. I can feel him growing hard against his jeans as my hips begin to move. God, I'm desperate for him. I've missed the way he holds me and the way he knows how to work my body. I crave the closeness to him.

"River," he groans as his lips travel down my jaw. "Keep working me up like that and I'm gonna fuck you right here on these bleachers for anyone to see."

"No one around," I tell him as I run my hands down his strong torso. His abs jump and flex, and then I find the button of his jeans. I kiss his cheek and then whisper in his ear, "Tell me to stop."

"Fucking never," he growls as his fingers dig into my ass.

Making quick work of his jeans, I pull his hard cock out of his boxers, stroking it between us. His head falls forward onto my collarbone as he breathes deeply.

"Oh, fuck." His breath is hot against my skin. "Ride me, darlin'. Let me feel you."

He lifts me up with ease, and as he tugs my panties to the side, I fall down onto his cock with one slow stroke. He fills me up, stretching me wide and hitting me deep in my core. We fit perfectly together.

"You like knowing anyone could walk in here and see us, firefly?" he asks as his hands cup my breasts through the soft fabric of my dress. "You like knowing anyone could see me claiming my woman?"

"Yes." I roll my hips, and my breath comes out in a hiss. He's hitting a deep, oh-so-sweet part of me. And the fact that we're out in the open, where anyone on the grounds could happen upon us, makes me even wetter. I like knowing he loves me so much he will claim me in front of anyone and everyone.

And I really like knowing he's so hard for me he can't wait until we're in private.

"That's it, baby." He fists my hair and tugs hard, forcing my head back so that he can kiss and lick my throat. The other hand slips between us to tease my clit, shooting off fireworks behind my eyelids. "So wet for me. Just for me."

"Just for you," I say as I pant with each thrust. I'm so fucking close already. I'm pent-up and needy as hell.

"When you come, firefly," he says while he keeps working my clit with his thumb, "I want you to shout my name. You hear me? You let everyone around here know you're mine."

Our bodies are smacking together, the wet noises echoing in the covered area.

"Fuck. I love you." He can feel that I'm on the edge,

ready to free-fall over it. His thumb circles, and I sink down hard on top of him, grinding so that he's as deep as he can be. "Come for me."

My body lights up, and my toes curl. I come, shouting his name so loud I'm sure people on the other side of the grounds heard me.

"You're squeezin' the life out of me." He lets go of my hair and tugs me in for a kiss, thrusting up into me as best he can with this angle as he comes.

"I like that face you make," I tell him with a smile as my finger goes between his eyebrows to smooth out the crease there. "Every time you come, you get so serious and concentrated."

"Because you damn near kill me each time," he says, slapping me hard on my ass. "Trying to make sure I don't pass out and miss the fun."

I laugh as he kisses me all over my face.

"You're so stupid."

"Stupidly in love with you."

"Cheesy." I grin and roll my eyes.

"Thanks for giving me a second chance, firefly."

"Technically, it was a third," I tease.

"Well, I guess it's true what they say, then." He takes my face in his hands and kisses me softly before pulling back, giving me a perfect view of those deep blue eyes. "Third time's a charm."

EPILØGUE

River

A couple of months later…

THERE'S a knock at the door, and Hayes is elbow-deep in his newest project: baking bread. His grandma used to make him grilled cheese sandwiches on her home-made bread, and he's had a craving for the past few weeks. Katherine tried to make it for him, but he's determined to learn by himself. So we've both just had to sit back and watch all of the failed attempts.

It's funny, but goddamn is it messy.

"I've got it!" I call out to him as I run down the stairs. I moved in with him shortly after the fair because there was really no avoiding it. It was inevitable that we would get here, and neither one of us wanted to be running back and forth on the property to be with one another. And Betty doesn't mind her new place a bit. She even takes naps with Hayes, lying right on top of him and tucking her little snoot into his neck.

"I think I've got it this time!" he calls back. "Dough feels right!"

"I have all the faith in you, babe."

I pull the door open, and Wells is standing there, soaked head to toe from the rain. His chest is heaving, and if it weren't for the stupid grin on his face, I'd think he was in trouble or something.

"Are you running from the cops?"

He groans and rolls his eyes.

"Gonna let me in?" he asks, peeking around my shoulder.

"Uh, yeah, of course. Sorry. Let me get you a towel or something, goodness' sake." I laugh as I step to the side. "Hayes, it's Wells!"

I run to the closet in the laundry room and pull out a fresh towel, tossing it to him as he stands in the foyer, trying to shuck his shoes off. He takes a second to dry off while I move to the kitchen.

"Drink?" I ask him as he walks in, drying his hair with the towel quite violently.

"Nah, I'm only here for a second. Just came from Rhett and Poppy's. You know they got married today?"

"Shut the fuck up!" I give his shoulder a hard shove. "She didn't tell me!"

"Probably want to tell you in person. They said

something about coming over tomorrow. So...act surprised?" He shrugs.

"So, why are you running around from house to house in the middle of a storm?" Hayes asks as he tries desperately to get all of the dough off his fingers and into the bread machine.

"Oh, right. Yeah. I have news." He wags his eyebrows at us.

"You're bein' a dick tease," Hayes grumbles. "Fucking out with it."

"Ignore him." I roll my eyes at Wells. "He's just pissy because he's been working on this bread for three weeks and still hasn't got it."

"I'm not pissy."

"You are," I tell him.

He sighs and abandons his mission. He closes the lid of the bread machine and moves to the sink to wash his hands instead. That's going to make a lovely mess in the drain stopper.

"You gonna tell us or what?" Hayes asks, drying his hands and leaning against the counter.

"I am dating someone. Have been for a while, actually." He smiles like a maniac. "Anyway, I'm telling you this because I need you guys to not be so shocked when you meet her and her family."

Hayes and I are both silent, just staring at him.

"I'm sorry...what?" My brain cannot compute.

"You're single..." Hayes looks like his brain might

explode.

"No," Wells says, his grin turning into a full-blown smile. "I'm not."

"I really need more information than what you are giving, dude." Hayes laughs. "You've been hiding some chick?"

"Don't call her *some chick*." I swat at Hayes.

"I'm just making the rounds to let everyone know. She's coming over tomorrow."

"Okay, well…awesome!" I wrap him up in a big hug because as confused as I am, it's still exciting.

"We are still missing so much information." Hayes laughs as he wraps both of us up in his arms. "But whatever. Can't wait to meet her!"

"Have you told Katherine and Clyde?" I ask as I try to escape the man sandwich.

"They're next." He jumps off the barstool and winks at me.

"Is there a reason this couldn't wait 'til the morning?" Hayes asks.

"Didn't want to." Wells shrugs.

"Wait!" I cut in before Wells makes it out the door. It's blowing and pouring the fucking rain down. "At least take a damn umbrella!"

"It's storming…" He looks at me like I've lost my mind. "You want me to carry a lightning rod?"

"Okay, fine. Good point. But good lord, be careful!"

His wide-ass smile is the last thing I see before he

dips out, leaving me and Hayes just staring at the door for a moment.

"Did that really just happen, or did I dream that?" I turn back to Hayes, who looks just as puzzled as I am.

"Wonder why he was hiding it?" Hayes asks, still staring at the door. "Think we know her?" His eyes light up. "Think it's embarrassing?"

"I think you should be happy for your brother." I boop his nose. "Whether or not you know her. But I'm guessing, with a town this small, we all know her."

The bread machine starts thumping on the counter, and Betty, who thinks the thing is her archnemesis, starts growling and barking at it.

"I don't think it should be doing that." I bite back my laughter because I know this is his new thing. I just wish he'd let someone help. He's going to break the damn thing.

"It shouldn't." He groans and takes off toward the kitchen, turning it off and sweet-talking Betty, calming her down.

I lean against the doorway and watch him with her. What is it about a dog dad that gets the blood going? I swear, every time I hear his baby talk or see them cuddling on the couch, my ovaries start acting up.

"Do you want kids?"

He stops in his tracks and turns to face me, an eyebrow raised.

"That seems out of the blue."

"It kind of is." I shrug. "But we've never really talked about it. I'm just curious."

He walks over to me and wraps me up in his arms, swaying me back and forth.

"I think I want anything you want."

"Hayes." I roll my eyes. "Kids aren't something you just have because your partner wants them. And I'm not saying I do…I'm just talking."

"I think I want you," he says, kissing my forehead. The way he's looking at me makes my stomach flip-flop. "I want you and everything that entails. I want to be married to you." He kisses my cheek. "I want to travel and grow old with you." He kisses my nose. "And if there's a baby or two in the midst of all that, that's fine with me."

"I've never really thought of myself as a mother."

"If there's no babies at all, that's fine with me, too." His lips find mine. "Like I said, I want anything you want. I want you."

"I think you'd make a great dad," I tell him earnestly. "I've seen you with Jo and Wade, and even with our sweet baby daughter." We both laugh. "I think it would be a shame to keep you from being a dad. That baby would be so loved."

"We don't have to decide right now, River. We can take each day as it comes. And if we get to a point later in life where we want kids but you don't want to put your body through that, we'll adopt."

"Are you trying to say when I'm *old*?" I poke his chest.

"When we're *both* old."

"Sounds like a plan, cowboy." I look up at him and rest my chin on his chest. "Now, can I *please* help you with this godforsaken bread?"

Want a sneak peek of Wells & Lennon? Keep reading to see how their story starts.
You can pre-order Roped now!

Lennon

He should be here by now.

I look around the crowd gathering in this tiny diner, and I feel suffocated. Everyone keeps looking at me, expecting my boyfriend to walk in any moment. It was a surprise when I told everyone that he was coming this morning, mainly because I've barely talked about him for the last nine months. All they know is that he's a man and we're dating.

I keep asking myself if maybe I'm hiding him for a reason. Am I embarrassed at how much older he is? Am I embarrassed that sometimes I look at him and I don't really find him all that attractive? God, maybe I'm subconsciously worried that they're all going to talk about us behind my back.

But honestly, they're probably used to it. I've always been the kind of person to keep my emotions and experiences to myself. I've never been the one to scream about things from rooftops. I don't know why

I've always been embarrassed to talk to my family and friends about that stuff. My sister gives us every juicy detail. Meanwhile, I'm over here barely letting you know what color hair he has. They don't even know his name.

I catch Mom's eye, and she gives me a sympathetic smile. A smile that says, "I'm so sorry, baby. Are you being stood up?"

Fuck. Am I?

Ryan's supposed to follow me this week, just ten days after I moved back myself. He's been packing his apartment, tying up loose ends, and getting the movers booked. From the very beginning of us talking, I made it very clear to him that my end goal was Cane Creek. That I didn't want to get into anything serious with anyone because of it. But he's been supportive from the get-go, telling me that he'd follow me if we got serious enough. And I took that as a green light.

My family is from Cane Creek, but my mom moved away after high school, wanting to experience big-city life instead of slow, small-town living. But she always brought us back to visit, never missing a single summer. Bill, my uncle, owns a bar here, and the rest of my family does mostly blue-collar work. So my mom is the black sheep of the family, running her own medical practice in the city over, about two hours away.

I fell in love with this place. I knew from the time I was a little kid that I would want to live here when I was older. This place has always called to me like a siren song, and since I work from home, I saved up the funds and moved back as soon as I could after graduation. And Ryan decided to make the move with me, taking our relationship to the next level: moving in together.

This is the first of many family get-togethers we'll be having over the next month as my sister prepares to get married up in the mountains. Why anyone would want to get married in Montana in the fall is beyond me. But here we are.

And Ryan is late.

I'm holding my phone so tightly in my hand that the damn screen might crack. But right as I'm about to text him *again*, the phone starts vibrating. I look down, and the anxiety melts away. Finally. He's calling.

"Excuse me," I say to the table. Then I turn to my mom. "He's calling. He might be lost."

I practically trip over three chairs on my way outside, rushing to make sure I can answer it before he hangs up.

"Hey!" I'm out of breath and rounding the corner for a little bit of privacy from the big glass front windows of the diner.

"Hey, Lennon." He sounds tired.

"You almost here? Get lost on the back roads?" I laugh a bit, teasing him because he's been talking about how he's never lived so far away from a Walmart.

"Look, I— uh." There's mumbling in the background that I can't quite make out, like he's covered the bottom of his phone or something. "Lennon, look. I can't make it."

"What do you mean?" My entire body flushes with heat, like I'm standing next to a bonfire. It's silent on his side except for him breathing. God, he always has been a mouth breather. "What do you mean?" I ask again, my voice angrier.

"I'm not— I'm not coming, Lennon. I— this whole thing. It's just too much for me. I'm staying in the city."

I think I'm hallucinating. I pull the phone away from my ear, look down at it to make sure it is actually connected to Ryan, and then put it back to my ear. I stutter, throw my hand over my mouth, and smile out of sheer shock, I think. Staring at the busy street in front of me, I take a few steps back, trying to get away from any witnesses. If I could reach through the phone and strangle this man right now, I think I would.

"Excuse me?"

He sighs. This man *sighs*. Like I'm the one putting him out.

"Lennon, I've met someone."

"I've been gone ten fucking days!" I whisper.

"It happened before you left. I didn't think it was going to amount to anything, but she's asked me to stay. And...I think I want to. I think I need to explore this before committing to you."

I am having a visceral reaction to this, like my body

refuses to accept the information he's giving me. Cannot compute, it says over and over again. And then my body just kind of stops working. My phone falls to the ground, and everything feels hot and cold at the same time. My rational brain knows what this is: a panic attack. I used to have them all the time in high school, but after steady therapy sessions and finding the right meds, they've all but disappeared.

But this is too much. My family is inside, waiting for me to introduce this man, and he's just told me that he's been cheating on me. I cannot go back in there and face that. I can't tell them that.

What the fuck. What the fuck. What the fuck.

My breathing becomes shallow, and I bend over, squeezing the life out of my knees as I try not to throw up. My vision is blurry, and my pulse is thrumming so loudly that I can't hear anything else. Including the person that is now standing in front of me. All I can see are his cowboy boots and the bottom of his jeans.

Until he squats down to be at my eye level. He says something, but I continue to stare at the ground. Maybe if I ignore him, he'll go away.

"Tell me what's wrong."

His commanding voice breaks through the panic seizing my throat.

"I'm having a panic attack."

"Okay." He slowly picks my phone up off the ground, the screen black now since Ryan probably hung up, and places it in his back pocket. "I'm only picking this up so that it doesn't sit in the dirt," he explains, his voice calm as my breaths come shorter and faster. "And now I'm going to squeeze you."

"You're going to what?"

I stand up straight just as his arms wrap around my body and fucking *squeeze*. He was not kidding when he said he was going to squeeze me. His body is huge compared to my short frame, and he lifts me off the ground as his gigantic arms suppress my nervous system.

Because of the way he's picked me up, my face lands right in the crook of his neck, and as the squeezing starts to take effect, I can't help but relax into it and take a little sniff because this man smells delicious. I mean, oh, my god. Like all my favorite man soaps merged into one mouth-watering scent just for me.

Between that and the crushing he's currently giving me, I start to calm down. My breathing returns to normal, and my heart rate starts to slow. I suck in a deep breath, and he carefully places me back on my feet. He doesn't let go quite yet, his arms still firmly wrapped around me.

"Better?" he asks, his voice deep and far too close to my ear. In fact, did I just catch him taking a whiff of me?

"Um." I clear my throat and try to pry myself out of his grip. "Yes. Thank you."

He takes a step back, finally giving me a good look at him. I've definitely seen him around before, which is bound to happen in a small town. His blond hair and dark brown eyes are a sharp contrast, but it works for him. Although, when you have a rancher's body and classic good looks, there's not going to be a lot that doesn't work for you.

"Here's your phone." His arm extends, and I take it back while trying not to touch him again. I'm feeling… overwhelmed. "Wells."

He's left his hand outstretched. I look at it and then back to his face, where his eyebrow is raised and a smirk tugs at the left corner of his mouth.

"Lennon." Guess we're past being touch shy. I take his hand and give it one firm shake before pulling my hand back to my side.

"Wanna tell me what happened, Lennon?"

"Oh, you know. Normal stuff. Boyfriend who was supposed to be moving in with me today just dumped me. Not only did he dump me, he also admitted to cheating on me. And did I mention that my entire family is waiting inside for me? For me *and him*?" I let out a loud, one-note cackle. "For the first time, by the way. This was supposed to be his grand entrance."

He doesn't look at me with pity, which is seriously appreciated. I'm already embarrassed enough at spilling all of this to a complete stranger after we had a very long, very intense hug.

"Alright." He moves his hands through his hair, fixing it over to the side to look a bit neater, and then unrolls his sleeves and buttons them at the wrist. Shame, honestly, because those forearms were really something to look at.

"What are you doing?" I ask when he starts tucking his shirt into his jeans.

"Becoming more presentable."

"Okay," I drawl. "But why?"

"They don't know him, right?"

"No." I narrow my gaze.

"Don't even know what he looks like?"

I shake my head slowly.

"Well… Can't let you go in and face that music alone, can I?" He winks at me, and then bends his arm in my direction. "Let's go, girlfriend."

ABOUT IVY JACKSON

Ivy Jackson is a lover of quiet small towns, nights where you can see all the stars, and the smell of hay being cut (even though it sends her allergies into overdrive). She grew up in a tiny village along the Ohio River where there was nothing better to do than ride four wheelers, go cow tippin', and get into far too much trouble at Friday night football games.

You can follow her on her socials:

Instagram & TikTok - @author.ivyjackson
Facebook Group - Ivy Jackson's Small Town Smuts

Or visit her website to get all the info, as well as signed copies and swag:

www.ivyjackson.com

ACKNOWLEDGMENTS

Thank you so much for reading Untamed! When I saw how my beta readers fell head over heels for Hayes, I knew he had to be our next brother. Him and River were so fun to write, and getting to show that Betty could make a comeback was one of the best parts.

I've worked with dogs a lot over the past ten years, and it always breaks my heart when people write off dogs who have a past. They just need the right owners and a lot of patience. And I'm glad I got to throw a little of that in this one.

Thank you to my alpha and beta readers for all of your time and feedback. I appreciate your endless patience as I threw chapter after chapter your way, even when it was way past when I said I would have it done.

Thank you to Sandra for always making my books the best they can be, and for knowing that when I say I'll have my manuscript to you by a certain time, I normally mean a week or two after that.

Thank you to Tori and Cady at Cruel Ink for always making my words and covers come to life. Thank you for last minute fixes and bookings. Thank you for your kindness. Thank you for being friends.

Thank you to Jillian who squeezed all of my discreet covers in last minute because I thought I had emailed you when I hadn't. I should really get better at checking my emails…

Thank you to Wander and Forest. The picture for the model cover was perfect, and I knew that the second I saw it!

Thank you to Julia for your endless support, even when I ask you for things last minute or do things without telling you first. Love you babe.

And always… thank you to Christopher. My husband. Thank you for letting me rest when I need it, and being proud of me when I do. Thank you for letting me talk about the sex scenes, and for letting me test out certain positions when I'm not sure if they'll work. Haha! Love you to the moon and back, stinky butt.